Th

Aerwyn of Atlantica

Maggie Jones

Copyright © 2018 Maggie Jones
All Rights Reserved.

2

Dedicated to my dad, who believed in The Mers from the beginning.

Chapter 1: The Arrivals

The day that the Pacificanans swam in their small and tired group to the City of Biscay, Aerwyn's home, her life changed forever. The day had started like any other day. Aerwyn had awoken early, and the morning sun was just starting to spread its fingers deep into the ocean to create its swirling stars on the sandy sea floor. She sat up, stretched her arms, and swung her tail over the side of her netted hammock.

Today, she thought, was going to be a wondrous day. She and Ula, her best friend since childhood, were going to spend the whole day reading the books that the traveling waresmer had sold to them yesterday. Aerwyn loved books. Mers did not have their own books. They told their stories by word of mouth, memorizing them so that they could pass on their histories, science, and art. The human books, however, required no such memorization. Preserved by those mers who would scavenge old shipwrecks, the books told of life outside of the water. That life sounded rough and unpleasant to Aerwyn, but she loved reading about the adventurous heroines who would find love in the big cities and vast landscapes of the land.

Aerwyn put her arms through a pale green long-sleeved shirt made of shimmering fish scales and pulled over a woven vest of dark green fish scales that she had made herself. It was a plain assembly, but Aerwyn thought the vibrant green went well with her hair and tail. Or rather, she thought it made her blend in more with the rest of the mers in Biscay because the outfit covered up most of her torso and arms. Aerwyn had long black hair that she braided in one hundred small braids to keep from tangling, a style many merwomen adopted since their human hair was not well-suited to the salty ocean water. Her skin was a very pale purple, and her tail, which started below her belly button, transitioned from skin to fish in a cascade of shimmering, vibrant, deep purple scales.

She eyed herself in the broken mirror scavenged from a shipwreck many years ago. As she sighed slightly, her grandmother poked her head into the room. "Aerwyn my dear, are you agonizing over that fabulous purple skin of yours again?"

Embarrassed, Aerwyn tossed her head, "Of course not grandmother, you know I don't care about that." Her grandmother smiled and left Aerwyn to her thoughts. She sighed. The truth is, grandmother, she thought to herself, you won't give me any answers about this purple, so I've given up.

The mers of Atlantica were of various shades of green. Their light green skin would accent their tails of a deeper shade, and their hair was always a color in between green and blue, never black. She looked at herself in the mirror again and dismissed her image. She felt like she would never completely fit in. The fish scales on her shirt helped her glide through the water, but they couldn't help her look like everyone else.

Aerwyn had given-up asking her grandmother, Coventina, about her different looks. All Coventina would tell her was that her parents were from away and did not lead their lives in the cold Atlantic waters, which required the green camouflaged skin. Coventina had different looks herself. She had white hair, pale white skin, and a magnificent rainbow tail that changed color with every flick or turn. This was because Coventina was a mermagician and had some of the old magic in her. There were a few mermagicians left in Atlantica, and they were discussed frequently in her history class at the Academy, so Coventina was able to swim around without any mers secretly wondering about her. There were no descriptions of purple mers in their histories, and, as far as Aerwyn could tell, she had none of that magic in her to explain why she looked different from the rest of the tribe. As much as she didn't let others' opinions about her personal appearance bother her, Aerwyn greatly desired to know why she was different. She couldn't shake the nagging recurring feeling that Coventina was hiding something from her.

Aerwyn selected one of her favorite headpieces from a basket in the corner of her room. It was a small silver circular band that fit around her head, with a green flower, carved from coral, on either side. Finally, she grabbed a necklace with several beads of bright red and pink coral hanging from it. There, she thought, I'm all prepared for a day of reading about adventures. She looked around her room to make sure it was tidy, a preventative measure against Coventina inserting herself into the room to tidy it herself. The room was small and cozy. Her hammock hung from the ceiling and was wide and comfortable. There were woven mats on the floor of various shades of pink and green seaweed, stacks of books on every surface, and, Aerwyn's favorite touch, strands of red, pink, green, and white coral beads hanging against the walls to give the space color. She turned from the arched doorway, closed the woven curtain, and glided into the main room, where her grandmother was at work stirring some form of algae stew. Coventina looked up from the pot and smiled warmly at Aerwyn. Her skin wrinkled around her bright eyes, revealing a long life that had been full of excitement. "Enjoy yourself my love" she said and looked back at the pot. Aerwyn patted her grandmother's silky white head and slid out the door.

They had been eating a lot of algae stew recently. Fish were becoming more and more scarce outside of Biscay, and the hunters foraging farther and father to bring less and less to the city. Aerwyn couldn't remember a time when she had been completely full. She put the thought to the back of her mind, today was supposed to be about adventure.

Ula lived about a six minute swim from Aerwyn. Her home was the biggest and in the center of the cliff. This was because Ula's mother, Ulayn, was the Queen of Atlantica. In the mer world, the leadership of communities passed down through the female line. Ulayn, who looked like she could be her daughter's twin with her dark emerald green fins and hair and pale green skin, was a shrewd, smart woman, who was already being declared "The Protector" for all of the work she was doing to find sustainable ways to continue Atlantica's once prolific agriculture industry. Ulayn made Aerwyn feel awkward and too fanciful. Although Ulayn was never anything but polite to her daughter's best friend, Aerwyn could tell that she didn't approve of them whiling away hours reading the human lore in the big cavernous library. Aerwyn suspected that Ulayn blamed her for her daughter's lack of interest in the community's agricultural needs.

Aerwyn swam to the front door and knocked on the giant, sea serpent headed knocker. It resounded, in the way that all sounds passed under the sea, with a slow, clanging echo. A finsman, dressed in the customary green vest and Atlantica crest of a red spiny sea urchin, came to the door and ushered Aerwyn inside. Since she was well known with the various finsmen on duty, it was always easy to slip into the massive home to find her friend. Aerwyn looked up at the cavernous ceilings of the entry hall, lit by thousands of bioluminescent algae trapped in cages, giving the room alternating green and red glows. Mers could see in the dark, but their night vision only picked out shapes and forms. A little light went a long way to knowing what was going on around you. Unlike most homeowners, who kept a single angler fish to light their homes in the evenings when the natural light was faded and the doors closed off to nighttime predators, the Queen lit her home in this artistic way. Aerwyn thought it was slightly depressing.

Aerwyn exited the cavernous entry way through a small hole in the rock wall and took off down the passage that led to the library, excited about the prospect of a long day of reading the wonderful novels housed there. The library in the castle was her favorite place on earth. What made it so wonderful was that it was built in the shape of a nautilus. When you entered the door, you swam in a spiral up and up and up, with rows of books all around you. Cozy little nooks for reading were cut in into the chambers and were outfitted with an angler lamp and comfortable woven cushions. However, Aerwyn's and Ula's favorite place was at the very end of the spiral. This chamber had windows that opened up to the outside waters, and natural light burst through, lighting the entire library. The openings also looked over the entire city and had a view like no other in the place. You could see the village mers going about their business two-hundred fins below. You could also see leagues beyond where the sharp continental slope led to deeper and darker waters, as well as up higher to the vibrant pastures of coral and seaweed of the coastal zone in which the mers had settled. Ula had beaten Aerwyn up there, and she looked up from her nest of pillows when Aerwyn arrived. It appeared from the smell wafting down the spiral, as well as Ula's mischievous grin, that she had stolen some ruby red kelp cakes for them to indulge in. This is going to be a perfectly luxurious day, thought Aerwyn.

The friends were just settling in to discuss their current human obsession, Robin Hood and the spunky Maid Marian, when they heard a commotion outside. Aerwyn stuck her head out the opening of the chamber and looked down the few hundred fins to the front door of the castle. A group of mers, clearly strangers due to their hair and fin color not the greens of Atlantica, floated waiting for entry. They must have just arrived, she thought, because she had not seen them when she had taken in the view just moments ago. Ula stuck her head out next Aerwyn, and in the typical, matter-of-fact and pushy Ula fashion, asked what was going on. Before Aerwyn could reason a guess, the finsmen below admitted the group of yellow and orange haired mers into the mansion. Aerwyn looked at Ula. Without speaking, they grabbed hands and swiftly glided down and down the spiral and out of the library. Turning immediately left they entered an empty and undecorated passage, covered in coral. As they usually did whenever they wanted to know what was going on, they moved one of the stalagmites aside and entered into a little chamber, that, through a tiny rock crevice, overlooked the parliament hall. The visitors were being led in by the castle guards.

As far as she could see from the crevice that provided a view into the hall where the parliament met, the mers that had arrived were five in number. There was a mermagician with the arrivals. He was much older than her grandmother, but he had the telltale long white beard and hair, both braided in a single braid, and the iridescent multicolored tail that hinted of the old magic the mer was capable of performing. Aerwyn could now tell that they were from the Pacificana tribe because, although she had never met the few Pacificana mers who had travelled through her city over the course of her 17 years, she had read about their blue tails, bright yellow or orange hair, and human colored skin. Aerwyn had learned that this skin pigment was due to the increased amount of sun in their ocean.

As they floated in the parliament hall, informally and casually kept in place by the finsmen swimming slowly around, the Pacificanans certainly looked bedraggled to Aerwyn. Their faces were drawn with exhaustion, but that did nothing to diminish their striking brightness in the well-lit main hall. The light streaming from the ceiling windows in the cavern lit up the hall and fell on the Pacificanans almost as if they attracted the silty light. Aerwyn could not take her eyes away from the glowing group.

There was a hubbub around the main hall door, and Ulayn entered with several mers who Aerwyn recognized as her advisors and most important finsmen. She was dressed in the traditional warrior garb of the Atlanticans, a silver circlet around her head, with matching bands around her arms, as well as a formal fitted vest, with strands of silver woven into the obsidian colored fish scales that made it shine when she moved gracefully through the water. The new mers graciously bowed their heads to her as she glided past to take her seat at the forefront of the room. Aerwyn shivered a little, as she always did in the presence of her best friend's intimidating mother.

"Welcome friends from the west to Atlantica, the Voyager Ocean," Aerwyn could hear Ulayn greet the guests, "it has been quite some time since our mers have had the opportunity to receive your tribe as guests." At this, a tall, lean mer moved forward and bowed his head.

"Queen Ulayn, thank you for receiving us and hearing our plea on such short notice." He turned to nod to each advisor and Aerwyn was able to get a better look at him. Aerwyn's first thought was that he could be very handsome, with bright orange hair and piercing dark eyes. He was slim but well-muscled, and his royal blue tail was long and full of strength. However, he had a sternness to his face that made him seem closed-off and unlikeable. "We have come here from our tribe in the Great Ocean as outlaws and accept refuge for a night within your walls. We also ask that you hear our proposition to your tribe."

Several other mers started filtering into the hall. Aerwyn noticed several of the prominent businessmers, the historian Lennes, several of the older mers. Coventina also flitted in, for which Aerwyn was not surprised, as she often advised Ulayn. Coventina's eyes briefly darted up to the crevice that Aerwyn and Ula were peering out of, making Aerwyn suspicious once again that Coventina had more magical powers than she protested. They must have sent word out fast, thought Aerwyn.

Ulayn opened her arms wide to the mer who spoke, indicating that he should continue speaking amidst the filtering in of other mers. "If you would like to gather the foremost of your tribe, I would be happy to wait," He said in response.

Ulayn smiled back at the mer and replied "please proceed young merman." The mer looked back at his bedraggled friends, as if to say, sorry, we can't rest yet, and launched into the tale of his travels.

"Queen Ulayn, I am Fenn of Pacificana, son of Queen Puk Puk and brother to Princess Puakai, the heiress to the Pacificana throne," he said, motioning to a very young mermaid behind him. "Your grace, the mers across the five oceans and seven seas are in grave danger. "

Chapter 2: The Pacificanans

When Aerwyn was a small mer, her grandmother would tell her tales of the old days, back when magic was prevalent and used to aid the humans. Mers and humans got along back then. They had a symbiotic relationship--the mers protected the humans from the sea, leading them from storms and rescuing them from their capsized ships when the violent swells became too much for their human vessels. Coventina would talk for hours about how her grandmother had once swam with a pirate for 17 hours before help arrived for him. Coventina would wink when she told Aerwyn this, giving Aerwyn the uncomfortable feeling that Coventina's grandmother had taken a fancy to the pirate. In turn, the humans respected the mers' hunting grounds and settlements, leaving them to rule the vast expanse of the five oceans and seven seas. Atlantica had been deemed the Voyager Ocean due to the vast amount of human and mer travel above and within its waters.

But those were the past times. Today, Aerwyn and the rest of the mers kept to themselves. It had proved too dangerous to interact with humans once they developed far-reaching weapons and a desire to capture the mers for display at their fairs and festivals. Too many mers had been lost, and no humans seemed to care about their pleas for respect and distance. So, the mers traveled deeper to the sea, further away from the fruitful gardens and forests of the shallow coastal zone and right to the edge of the continental shelf, on the brink of the dangerous deep seas. There, life was harsher and darker for the mers. While the cold and dark did not affect their cold-blooded bodies, it did limit the amount of sustenance available to the tribes as many of the foods they relied on needed the sun only available in shallower waters. At the edge of the continental shelf, they were closer to the larger predators that were always a looming threat.

One history that had been passed down from mer to mer, preserving itself in the minds of descendants and related through the oral traditions of the tribe, was the Tale of the Five Eldoris. The tale started the same way for every tribe: long ago the mers and humans coexisted peacefully. The story described the now myth-like relationship between the two species. The humans would explore the oceans and travel the world in their wooden and iron ships, and the mers would guide them to safety, out of storms and into calmer winds. For repayment, the humans didn't interfere with mer life, and did not impose their rule of law on the mers, leaving them to govern themselves. The sea was for the mers and the land was for the humans. The way the history goes is that, starting several hundred years ago, the humans stopped upholding their end of the deal. Too many ships started sailing the seas, and it was impossible for the mers to see them all to safety. More and more tales of merwomen being kidnapped for wives started surfacing. It was true that often merwomen or men would leave the sea for a life on land, with the help of a mermagician, but the involuntary exodus left the mers in constant fear, as well as depleted their ever shrinking population.

All of this came to a head in 1756 when the beautiful and beloved Pacificana princess, Reita, was kidnapped by a human sea captain, only to die shortly after when the captain and crew left her on board without any water to sustain her thirsty body. Her lifeless form was dumped unceremoniously into water, and no mermagician could raise her. King Reit called a meeting of all of the leaders of the five ocean tribes, the Pacificana, his tribe, the Atlantica, the Arcticana, the Indiansi, and the Southerns, collectively called the Five. According to the legend, the five leaders convened at a secret location and spent days arguing about the best course to take with the humans. Some wanted to continue to work with the oceans. This group included the Atlanticans. Others wanted nothing to do with them. This groups was led by the Pacificanans. Eventually, the Atlanticans were out-voted, and they joined the

Five reluctantly. The Five used some now forgotten, ancient magic to create a protection against the humans. In legends, this gathering became to be called The Five Eldoris.

The spell of the Five Eldoris engulfed all of the mers around the five oceans in an invisibility that they could not shed. This meant that they were undiscoverable by humans. It also meant that the mers could not interact with the humans at all--they could not get near, even to rescue a drowning child. Not even if they wanted to. No one knew very much about the kind of magic that was used. Only the mermagicians would speak of it, and they rarely did anymore. It was rumored that mermagicians, while unable to be seen by humans, could see them. As such, a law was passed in the early 1800s that sentenced any mer who interacted with humans to death. This law targeted the mermagicians, as they were the only ones who could still interact with humans. There was a slew of mermagician executions during the years following the passage of the law, and the mermaids and men gifted with magic were killed off to a very small number. Coventina was a descendent of a surviving mermagician of that time.

Since that last gathering, the tribes gathered into themselves. No longer interested in a life of service to the humans at sea, they became more interested in their own affairs. Universal gatherings for the Five stopped being held regularly, for there seemed to be no shared interests in the wellbeing of the others. This was the life that Aerwyn knew. A life that involved allegiance to the tribe and not to the whole ocean. A rugged individualism that all should look out for themselves ran the Atlanticans prior to Ulayn's rule. To Aerwyn though, the histories that Coventina shared with her made the prior life seemed wonderful. Adventures, rescue missions, and a reason for being were the underlying missions of the mers of old. Today, all Aerwyn could see was faded adventure and fear of the unknown. Even the mers' magic seemed to be fading. Coventina, who once had very strong powers that could make a wave stand still, now focused her magic on healing small mers' childhood wounds.

It was of the Eldoris that this stone-faced, magnum-haired mer was speaking. As the merman who had introduced himself as Fenn spoke, Aerwyn listened in rapt attention, physically aware of Ula doing the same by her side. "Our people can no longer withstand the human interference to our waters and indifference to our existence," Fenn stated, looking around at the mers gathered in the hall both in earnest and defiance, tempting them to interrupt him. "We Pacificanans have suffered from the rising temperatures and the overfishing. Our people are having difficulty reproducing. And, when they do, the chances that the young will make it past infancy are steadily decreasing. We can no longer withstand this ignorant exclusion of the humans in our world. We must work together with them to ensure our waters can remain. We must establish travel, fishing, and waste rules that will protect us from our land neighbors. We need to speak with the humans to do this. We need the humans to agree to our terms. If we don't do this, our whole race will perish in the next one hundred years." Fenn turned to the old mermagician and nodded his head slightly at his companion.

The mermagician swam forward and spoke in a gravelly, antiquated voice: "This is true. I have studied the effects of living without human regulation in our tribe for many years, and I would assume that the same losses are happening here." He looked at Ulayn directly when he spoke. "I brought my research to the leaders of Pacificana, and they disagreed. They did not think our survival depended on cooperation with the humans. Queen Puk Puk admonished me and told me she would rather all the mers die than be in allegiance with the humans. The scars from the death of Princess Reita still are fresh for our people, even after all of these years. But, this cannot be the opinion of all mers. There are none alive today who lived in a time when we worked hand-in-hand with the humans to preserve our planet. We personally cannot recall the treacheries, and we need to give the alliance second chance. It is risky, and certainly we need to find the right humans to present our plea to. But, we need to work together to do this as one tribe can't take on this weighty task alone."

A middle-aged advisor floating to the left of Ulayn put his hand up, "Sir, we too have experienced losses over the years. We too can see that it is from the humans fishing in and travelling in our waters. But how do you propose we bridge this gap? The old magic prevents any of us from contacting the humans."

The mermagician nodded slowly and sagely as he responded to the advisor. "I have researched this as well. We need to reverse the spell that created that barrier between our peoples." With that statement, the mers in the great hall started talking amongst themselves, some in anger and some in excitement. Aerwyn saw that Coventina had not taken her eyes off of the mermagician. "I believe" he said raising his gravelly voice over the growing noise of the crowd, "that we do this by holding another Eldoris. We must gather all of the heirs, the futures of the Five, along with the objects of the Eldoris, and reverse the spell." At this, his voice was drowned out by the gasps and whispers of the crowd.

The objects of the Eldoris? Aerwyn looked quizzically at Ula. She had never heard of those before. Ula looked back with a look that reflected Aerwyn's own lack of understanding. They turned back to the tumult below. Ulayn was holding up her hands, attempting to quiet the crowd. Once the noise fell to a humming murmur, she questioned the old mer, "Sir, how do you suppose to gather the Five. Even if you could manage to find the heirs and the Eldoris and actually convince them to participate, that is a very dangerous journey. Our seas are no longer populated enough to protect travelers from the harms along the way. That would be many days and nights of unprotected travel through deep seas."

The mermagician nodded in acquiescence, and stated, a little more tiredly than he had before, "that is true Queen Ulayn. The journey to unite the Five will be treacherous, and it does not come with the promise of agreement that any of the leaders will turn over their heirs and their Eldoris. We already know that, as we had to leave under the cover of secrecy with the heiress and our Eldoris, outsmarting our own warriors to the edge of the Panama Canal, and then making that treacherous journey through." He paused for a moment and then proceeded "it does not appear that they have… successfully… followed us here." He paused again, and looked straight at Ulayn. "It is a risk, I believe, that must be taken… we, even across the distance of the waters between us, have heard of you and your fair rule. We have heard you are called the Protector. We come to you first. If we cannot convince you, we can have no hopes that any of the other tribes will follow."

Ulayn leaned forward and, very briefly, uncharacteristically put her head to her hands. Every mer in the room had their eyes on her. She then leaned back, arms on her throne and eyed the mermagician with the sidelong slanted look that always terrified Aerwyn. "How do I know you are telling the truth? That your intentions are in fact to convene with the humans to save our people, instead of selling us off for profit?"

The mermagician smiled sadly, "I have only my word Queen." At this, the little princess Puakai, who could not be more than eight years old, with bright orange and yellow hair that seemed to change color when she moved, came forward.

"Queen Ulayn, if I may speak," she said, and then added once Ulayn gave her a kind nod, "I am the heiress to the Pacificana waters. In Pacificana, as is here, the leadership passes from mother to daughter. I have understood this since I can remember. I have not taken the responsibility lightly. I am not here as a captive. I am here of my own free will, for I will be the one ruling our people when the end comes. I will be the one who may not have a child survive past infancy due to the warming seas. I will be the one to see my people die of starvation. We have come to you to ask for your allegiance. We ask you for your Eldoris… and we ask you for your daughter."

The hall fell silent. Aerwyn reached out for Ula's hand, and Ula gripped her hard. They watched from above for several agonizing minutes that seemed like hours as Ulayn's bowed head conversed with her advisors. Occasionally she would nod slowly. This went on for just a few agonizing minutes that felt stretched into hours for Aerwyn. When it seemed like the crowd was about to burst in its silence, Ulayn rose up. Her facie revealed nothing. With a quick look up to their crevice, indicating that, in addition to Coventina, she also knew of their viewing point, she spoke to the hall. "Guests and new friends, my people and my old friends, I cannot say that I am surprised that it has come to this finally. The Atlanticans will join you in your quest."

Aerwyn heard Ula's sharp intake of breath, as she herself had stopped breathing.

Chapter 3: Preparations

Aerwyn stared at Ulayn through the rock crevice. She could feel Ula staring at the side of her face. She didn't know what Ula was feeling right now, but she thought that she must be feeling fear, and perhaps anger. She knew that if her unknown mother had volunteered her to travel through dangerous seas with a group of strangers, without consulting her, she would be upset, to put it mildly. She steadied her face and turned to her friend. Ula did not look fearful. She looked enraged. She grasped wordless at Aerwyn's arm.

"It's going to be okay, Ula." Aerwyn tried to reason, to her friend as well as herself. "Your mom wouldn't do this if she knew it was unsafe."

"Yeah right" seethed Ula. "You've met my mom."

They sat there for what seemed like ten minutes, without saying a word, Ula breathing heavily through her gills. Finally, Aerwyn felt they must move, if just to shake off the shock. They should probably go down there too she thought, if only to let Ulayn see the flesh and blood she was sacrificing to this group of strangers. She tugged at Ula's arm. Ula didn't seem to register that Aerwyn wanted her to move. "Come-on Ula, let's go down."

The friends creeped out from behind the coral wall, placed the stalagmite back in place, and quickly darted through the passageways, making their way to the front door of the parliament. Ulayn gave them a passing glance when they entered and hovered near the back wall, but did not otherwise appear to register that they had entered.

The conversation in the hall had turned into a negotiation. The mermagician and apparent group leader was listing the provisions that they would require. It seemed as if the voyage from the Pacific Ocean had left them with very little except that which they could hunt and forage. Now that she thought of it, Aerwyn could tell that their bodies were incredibly slim, and their eyes gave away great hunger. Was it just hunger for food that they contained? She wondered.

After engaging in several minutes of deep discussion with her advisors, which caused Ula to become increasingly restless next to Aerwyn, Ulayn addressed the travelers. "You shall have provisions, as well as several of my mers to travel with you for the protection of my daughter. Also, I will give you three of my great conch shells and some sea horses to drag them for you, so that you will not run short of supplies again. I appreciate the great risk that you have taken in coming here, and I am happy that our ocean can be an ally with your cause. I will request one term from you, however, before we can proceed." The Pacificanas stole glances at each other when she said this. "I will request," bellowed Ulayn so that the whole clan could hear her, "that in exchange for our support and participation in this quest, no mer blood shall be shed. No valuable and rare mer lives shall be taken in this venture, except in defense of a deathly attack on your group."

Without hesitation, the mermagician, matching her volume, cried out "Aye! We have a deal!" The female Pacificanan did not seem so happy about this, thought Aerwyn, as she turned her head to scowl at the ground.

By the look of her hand gestures, Ulayn appeared to be working out amongst her advisors who should go on this journey. There were several finsmen and women who had stepped forward to volunteer. Eventually Ulayn settled on Figgs and Folander, two brothers, slightly older than Aerwyn, who had been finsmen and part of the combing crew for several years. They were rugged and experienced looking and did not at all seem daunted by the task at hand. After she announced their names to the crowd, she stated "for the final mer joining this crew, I select Coventina, our mermagician, to bring her wisdom, skill, and knowledge of magic to this quest."

Aerwyn's heart stood still, both fearful and just a tiny bit envious at the same time, she frantically looked for her grandmother's white head in the mass of green. Her searching eyes finally rested on it bobbing at the front of the crowd. The head bowed to Ulayn. "Dear Queen," Coventina called out, loudly so that everyone could hear. "I fear that I am too weathered to take on this journey… I would only be a burden to the great adventure." She paused, and Ulayn gave her a knowing smile, giving Aerwyn an uncomfortable feeling that slowly started leaching its way into her skin. The feeling that some secret had passed between them. Coventina continued, "I ask that, in my place, you could accept my granddaughter."

For the second time that hour, Aerwyn had stopped breathing. She could not understand what was happening. It was all too much in a short period of time. Leave Biscay, she thought? Travel through the oceans? How could Coventina volunteer me for this without consulting me first? She is no better than Ulayn! Her bubble of wonder and fury was interrupted by the stern Pacificanan Fenn who had first addressed Ulayn.

"Excuse me, honorable mermagician, does this granddaughter have your same powers?"

Coventina's kindly face turned to the red-haired mer "she does not young sir."

"Is she a skilled warrior?" he asked.

"She is not."

"Is she a healer?" he asked, becoming impatient.

"She is not."

"Is she a scholar?"

"No"

"Does she have any skills at all?" he demanded.

"She is kind and… thoughtful," answered Coventina, "and she is so in the face of adversity."

"Psht. Thoughtful? She is useless. We don't want her. This is dangerous enough as is, we don't need someone without any skills dragging us down. Nice isn't an effective addition to this group," he stated harshly. "We are happy to take your finsmen, your heir, and any fighters--but this isn't a vacation."

Aerwyn blushed deeply at this. Never before had someone so articulately pointed out that she had no useful skills. And in front of so many Atlantican mers. She wanted to curl up inside herself and never show her face again.

"She is going" interrupted Ulayn, rising, for the first time ever, to her daughter's friend's defense. "We need to attend to our preparations--you shall depart in the morning." The orange-haired mer was flustered and angered by this, and he looked as if he was about to say something back to Ulayn when the mermagician quickly swam up to him and put his hand on his arm. Fenn gave him an angry look and then swam quickly and silently out of the parliament.

--

As the seat of the Atlantica tribe, the City of Biscay used to be a bustling metropolis where mermen and merwomen would come to attend the Academy, trade their wares, or attend to any business that was not supported by the outlying villages. However, the population of the city, reflecting that of the mers in general, had been decreasing precipitously in the past three hundred years. The City was built into the cliffs rising from the sands of the continental shelf. Coventina's home was similar to the hundreds of other mer homes. Small doorways carved into the cliffs, protected by thatched doors or curtains, that opened into cavernous homes inside.

As Aerwyn glided past these homes, swimming silently with Coventina, her face still warm and dark from what the Pacificanan had said, other mers were going on with their days as if nothing had changed. There were little anemone and seaweed gardens on most of the ledges and outcrops near the doorways in the cliff. One older merwoman opened her door as

Aerwyn passed, gave her a warm smile and wave, and, with a flick of her tail, floated up to the garden ledge above her doorway. Aerwyn watched her as she fingered the different algae growing there, prodding them to see if they were yet ripe enough to eat. As she floated by some small mer girls, she saw them eyeing her tentatively. One of the girls even grabbed at her friend's hand, perhaps for reassurance. When Aerwyn was small, Coventina would tell her that these looks were because she was so beautiful that no one knew what to do. Now, Aerwyn rolled her eyes at that thought. It hadn't taken her long to realize that these looks were due to her dark hair and purple fins. Just because she was used to it didn't mean she liked it, and Aerwyn flicked her tail with strength, as much a message to the mers that she didn't care what they thought as to glide past them.

It wasn't until they were in their homey cave that Coventina spoke. She sat on a rock, laying her satchel of healing sea herbs to the side. "My love," she said in a calm yet wearied voice, "I did not mean to speak for you." Aerwyn did not know how to respond to that and did not have time to before her grandmother continued. "It's just that… well… you are the right one to go on this trip. The journey will not require magic as much as it will perseverance and courage. I am an old mer, and although I wish I might have those desired traits hiding in the folds of my wrinkles, I do not have the strength to execute them. I spoke for you because I was afraid you wouldn't speak for yourself."

Aerwyn still did not know what to say. There was a swelling ball of anxiety in her stomach, but she wanted more than anything to rise to the occasion after her public humiliation. But she didn't rise to the occasion in front of her wrinkled and loving grandmer. "What do you always say grandmer? Ask for what you want and say what you don't want? Well, I'm going to do that." She tried to keep her voice low and calm, but it began to waver with emotion, "I don't want this! I don't want to leave our home."

Coventina smiled warmly at her. "I am sad to part with you. But, it is time for you to have one of those adventures that you're always reading about. With Ula. You two can do it together."

Aerwyn broke into tears. She couldn't not do it, she knew, especially since Ulayn had announced it to the whole tribe. She spoke through her tears "I want to want to go."

"Give it some time, my love, you will be glad you went." Coventina replied. But Aerwyn wasn't so sure of that at all, and the anxiety of the unknown overwhelmed her as the tears came fast and strong.

After some time Coventina extricated herself from Aerwyn's embrace and suggested they start packing in order to do something constructive. They were ordered to leave at daybreak, and Aerwyn didn't want anyone to see the evidence of her worry in her teary red rimmed eyes. As they packed throughout the evening, finsmen from the parliament came in and out with detailed instructions, directing her what to pack and what to prepare for. Coventina packed Aerwyn's collection of maps of the five oceans, her book of "Atlantic Plants and Fishes, a Practical Guide," as well as several short sleeve and long sleeve vests. Ulayn was going to provide the food and sleeping provisions, so all of Aerwyn's belongings fit in a sling that Aerwyn was to wear on her back, with one strap across her chest. One of the finsmen had brought her a small dagger and another brought her a spear to strap to her back. He briefly walked Aerwyn through the self-defense moves she had learned as a young mer but had long since forgotten from disuse.

Aerwyn did not get to bed until just a few hours from dawn. She settled into her hammock, savoring its familiarity. Like most fish, mers could control their buoyancy in small degrees.

She had to be taught as a young mer how to use the air bladder in her tail. Now, as a fully grown mer, the act was second nature to her. When she wanted to sleep, she merely allowed herself to sink into the hammock. Aerwyn looked at her cozy room around her, giving it the loving attention of a goodbye, and soon drifted into a restless sleep.

At some time in the night, Aerwyn couldn't tell when, she awoke to the sound of hushed voices, drifting slowly through the thick sea water of her home. At first, she thought the voices were part of her restless and weird dream that she was in a swim race and seemed to have lost the use of her tail and had to swim the rest of the course with only her arms, her schoolmates laughing at her. As she shook her head groggily, it became clear that the voices were coming from the main room. Curious, Aerwyn slid her tail over the edge of her hammock and propelled herself to the curtain that separated her room from the main room. Peeking out, making sure the curtain didn't move, Aerwyn could see Coventina sitting close to the Pacificanan mermagician. Closer up, he looked even older than she had initially thought. If Coventina is too old to take this swim, then he is certainly too old, Aerwyn thought. She strained her ears to hear what they were talking about, but after a few minutes of this she realized her attempts were futile. Both mers wanted their conversation to be private and were ensuring that even Aerwyn could not overhear them. Wracked with curiosity, Aerwyn tossed and turned for the rest of the evening.

Aerwyn was awoken from her restless sleep by Coventina much earlier than she was used to. Coventina had made a large breakfast of jellied clams and spiced jellyfish cakes that smelled delicious and that tasted even better. Aerwyn hunched over her meal, staring off into space, trying to wake-up her mind completely, as well as trying to gather her courage for this day. She thought over the events from the day before and how a regular day at the library had changed to her leaving Biscay for the first time ever. The instructions that Ulayn had sent over had been copious in her expectations of Aerwyn being a representative for the tribe. They also caused the anxiety ball in her stomach to grow because Ulayn was also depending on Aerwyn to protect Ula. The instructions also reminded her that she would be using her hunting and fish defense training, and that she was partly chosen for this role because of the excellence and speed in swimming that she had demonstrated in school. But the instructions also said confusing things, like "do whatever you must to achieve this purpose," and "do not waver from the course." Those words made Aerwyn feel anxious, and she pushed those feelings down into her belly where she didn't have to think about them. But as she pushed the feelings down, the tears welled-up again. Get a handle of yourself Aerwyn, she said to herself.

Just as the light started to fade into Aerwyn's home, with its yet tenuous fingers announcing the coming morning, Coventina said it was time for her to go. Unable to help herself, Aerwyn broke into sobs, resting her head on Coventina's shoulder, trying to speak through her tears.

"What if this is the last time I see you Coventina?" Aerwyn sobbed.

"Don't be silly love," Coventina soothed, stroking Aerwyn's braided black hair, "You, Ula, and the rest will be able to make it to the other tribes, or at least send messages for them to meet up with you, and be back her in no time. Think of it as one of those adventures in those human books you read."

It took a while for Aerwyn to stop crying, for she loved her grandmother dearly, and the thought of being separated from her, even for a few months, was hurting her heart. Eventually she was able to speak without sobbing, albeit in a wavering voice that embarrassed her a little, "I'll miss you so much Coventina, and I love you so much."

"Oh, Aerwyn, the same to you my love." Coventina extricated herself from Aerwyn's grasp and said "I have one more thing for you for the trip." Coventina reached around her neck and untied the string that held the iridescent coral pendant that she was never without. Holding the coral in her hand, she explained "This, Aerwyn, is the Atlanticans' Eldoris. This object holds the power to reverse the spell of the Five. But also, Aerwyn, it can be used with the Five to cast new, powerful spells, and it could be dangerous if in the hands of the wrong mer. Ulayn has instructed me to give this to you, and that Ula will be wearing a decoy Eldoris. If ever you get the whiff that this plan of the Pacificanans is not what they say it is, you, Ula, and the rest of the Atlanticans need to leave as soon as you can, and make sure that this Eldoris does not get into their hands."

Aerwyn took the iridescent coral from Coventina, twirling it around in her hand. It was beautiful. It was both clear as the seas as well as full of all the colors at the same time. She must have been transfixed at the twirling coral for several moments, for when she looked up, Coventina was holding Aerwyn's pink and red coral necklace and reaching to take the Eldoris back from Aerwyn. With the removal and replacement of a few of the coral beads, Coventina added the Eldoris to the necklace.

Next to the pink and red coral pieces, the Eldoris picked up their colors so that it looked like one, slightly special, coral bead on the strand. Then, Coventina fastened the necklace around Aerwyn's neck. "It's time, love." Coventina said, and Aerwyn could tell from her strained tone that she was not as excited about Aerwyn's adventure from Atlantica as she put on. She grasped Aerwyn to her in a hug and said fiercely, "No matter what happens Aerwyn, know that in your kindness and thoughtfulness is not a weakness. It is a strength. Use it." She smiled, "and of course, ask for what you want and say what you don't want." Aerwyn rolled her eyes at the advice she had heard from her grandmother a thousand times but hugged her even more tightly.

When Aerwyn arrived at the castle in the early light, it appeared as if she were the last one to arrive. Ulayn was present, and giving a formal farewell as Aerwyn sidled up to Ula. Hugs were given all around, and then they were off.

Chapter 4: Adventure Commences

Ulayn had provided the group with three of her giant conch shell carriages to haul the provisions, with four harnessed seahorses to pull each through the strong currents of the Atlantic Ocean. Aerwyn could see that the polished shells had stores of food for the journey--packed kelp, jars of red flaky dulse, alaria cakes, assorted sea vegetables, and jars upon jars of jellied clams. She could even see a box of the spiced jellyfish cakes that the chefs of the palace made best. There were camp supplies, hammocks, hunting spears and bows, and various other tools packed in and tied down onto the shell. Aerwyn felt a pang for the little horses carrying the laden shell, but they seemed to be full of rigor comfortable with the weight.

The group was pretty quiet for the first few hours of swimming. The Pacificanas were not particularly welcoming, which was surprising given their desperation to have the Atlanticans join them. As for the Atlanticans, Aerwyn had the sense that they had all gotten into something huge on a bit of a whim. Aerwyn stuck by the two finsmen that Ulayn had sent to protect Ula, Figgs and Folander. They had been a few years older than Aerwyn in school and had graduated from the Academy three and four years ago respectively, while Aerwyn still had one year left. Folander had a wife and a little mer. They lived near Aerwyn and Coventina, and she had seen them playing on the ledge outside of their home. Figgs was a comber, one of the patrolling mers who protected the City of Biscay from the likes of sharks and other dangerous predators. One time he had actually travelled to the Americas side of the Atlantic Ocean and had hand-to-hand combat with a man-o-war. Both of the brothers seemed excited to be on this trip and to put to test the skills they had learned during their years of training as finsmen. Ulayn had never before approved of a trip so far from Atlantica's capitol.

The Pacificanas on the other hand, should be more optimistic due to gaining Queen Ulayn's support for the quest of joining the Five Eldoris, seemed apprehensive and wary of their new companions. All, excluding Lachlan, a very long, broad-shouldered mer with yellow hair and a green tail. Aerwyn thought he must be close to her own age, 19, but she was not sure. His laugh made him seem young, but his strong body revealed a seasoned comber. He was friendly with the newcomers, and was the only one who spoke to Aerwyn for that first morning. In addition to Lachlan, there was Princess Puakai and her brother Fenn, the mermagician, who Aerwyn had learned was named Earendil, and a merwoman, Akemi, around middle age, also a comber.

Aerwyn could see why Fenn had been so concerned about her skill set in joining this quest. If most of the party was comprised of combers, and the rest were royalty or mermagicians, then she really didn't fit in at all. She also felt the old discomfort of being out of place when her practiced eye picked-up on the Pacificanas covertly examining her black hair, lavender skin, and bright purple tail. Unlike the little mers she had encountered growing up however, they were far too polite to say anything about it. Aerwyn fingered at the Eldoris on the chain of coral around her neck, looking at Ula. Coventina had made Aerwyn promise to keep the Eldoris a secret, but she thought that Ula must know, as she was wearing the decoy, a circlet of white sparkling coral, around her head.

As they swam along an old path out of the city limits, the mermagician Earendil gave the newcomers a layout of the Pacificanas' basic plan for the first part of the venture-- acquiring the five Eldoris and five heirs to the oceans. Since they already had two, their plan was to travel to the Arctic Ocean to gain the allegiance of Queen Skari. Although the Atlanticans and Pacificanas had always had an allegiance at best and working relationship at worst, the Arcticana had not participated in any communal mer events or decisions since the last gathering of the Five several hundred years ago. They had the reputation of sticking to themselves. In fact, Aerwyn had met a scarce few Pacificana, Indiansi, and Southern travelers in Atlantica throughout the years, she had never met any mer from that harsh sea in the north. Earendil informed the group that his reasoning in approaching the Arcticana before the remaining tribes was make a plea to Queen Skari's ego, that they could not do it without her. He said this in an almost triumphant way that made Aerwyn wonder whether every mer in the group had agreed with this approach. From there they would either send word or travel in person to the Indian Ocean and then the Southern Ocean to gather the remaining Eldoris. With Queen Skari's cooperation, it was unlikely the other two tribes should not follow. The mermagician seemed to think that the whole venture would take two months.

--

That first day, the mers swam about 20 miles, which was the furthest Aerwyn had ever been from her home. The group kept the far-off mountains of the Mid Atlantic Ridge to their left. The vegetation did not change from the seaweed and corals that Aerwyn was familiar with, but there were more fish about, the further they got from the center of Biscay. About one mile from the heart of the city, the mer homes, set up in the cliffs of the continental shelf thinned out, and just five miles out there were no longer signs of mer life. They traveled close to the ocean floor, as it provided them with the most protection from the fierce predators of the sea lurking above, but they did not meet with any harmful beasts that first day.

As they glided through the sea grasses blanketing this particular stretch of sea floor, and moved to and fro to avoid colliding with the large rocks and brain coral piled up on the floor, it appeared to Aerwyn that there was a trail here, albeit a bit overgrown. Thinking that this would be a good chance to start a conversation with the approachable Lachlan, Aerwyn slowed her pace until Lachlan, who was guiding the seahorses through the maze of rocks and coral at the end of the mer train, caught up with her.

"It's Lachlan, right?" Said Aerwyn tentatively and smiling hard in an attempt to be friendly.

Lachlan looked up from his task with a wide smile powering through his bushy yellow beard "Hey, yeah, it is. You're Aerwyn?" "

Yes!" Aerwyn smiled brightly, "I was wondering if this might be an old trail?" she responded. And so, the two started talking about the trail and how it was likely a major route back when the Five would regularly travel to and from each other's tribe capitols. This turned to other conversation topics, and Aerwyn found that the last miles of the day passed pleasantly along after she became comfortable talking to the large and boisterous mer. She found it took no time at all to gain that level of comfort, as he was very open and welcoming, and she rose to the occasion with her own natural openness.

The light was just beginning to fade into the long fingers of the evening sun when Earendil called a halt. The place he had chosen for their camp was a small circular space, off the trail, protected on all sides by large stones with just a small crevice to fit in and out of. The space above their heads was open to any predators, so they would have to have someone keep watch throughout the night. Lachlan led the little seahorses with their large cargo to the far side of the circle. He pulled off the ropes from the seahorses' harnesses, and let them free to flit about and stretch. It was unlikely that they would swim too far from the camp as they had been domesticated and knew that they would be getting their dinner with the mers. Aerwyn, Ula, Fenn, and Puakai unloaded the conch shells, as the rest scouted the area for potential dangers.

The shells, which had been laced down to keep the stores from flying out during the trip, held more than Aerwyn had initially supposed. Inside, there were hammocks for each of the nine mers, angler fish lamps, and some algae torches, along with the food provisions. Aerwyn set her hammock up next to Ula's, and dug into her satchel to take stock again of what she had packed. Ula was doing the same thing. This act made Aerwyn strangely comfortable, like they were just going on an Academy camping trip like they used to as young mers. The playfulness of those trips was not present with this group however. When Aerwyn thought about it, Ula had been really quiet today. Aerwyn was worried that she was stressed. How selfish am I to be so worried about this trip? I don't even have to do anything, she thought to herself. To try and relax her friend a bit, as well as herself, as her own anxiety was waiting to bubble over in her belly, Aerwyn swung her tail up on to the hammock, took a relaxed pose, and sighed "day one of Aerwyn and Ula's all-inclusive vacation to the majestic scenery and delicacies of the north complete." She looked over expectantly at Ula, who smiled back gratefully.

"This is not a vacation" a stern voice to her right said, and Aerwyn turned her head to see that Fenn, who was helping his little sister assemble her hammock, had overheard her joke and was staring icily at her. "Oh, um..." said Aerwyn, great she thought, that was bad timing. "I was just joking, of course this isn't a vacation." and then added "If this was a true vacation, I would be surrounded by dancing mermen, and there might be a bit more sunlight." Her smile faded as Fenn turned away without a response beyond a sour look. Her stomach made the usual clench when she thought someone was mad at her. To her surprise, Ula interjected as well.

"Aer, must you always be joking?" she said in her usual unadorned, brash way.

Aerwyn felt hurt. "I'm just trying to ease the tension." A few moments passed. "I'm stressed."

"Sorry," Ula responded quickly but not a bit sheepishly, they had always been pretty up front with each other about their feelings. Being competitive swimmers at the academy had brought them very close together, and they were able to express themselves to each other regarding the good and the bad. Nothing made you have to be honest like racing your best friend and having your tail whipped by them. "I shouldn't have snapped. It's just… well... I feel like I have no idea what is going on. My mom wouldn't really tell me anything, and I have the feeling that we were signed up for something more serious than we know."

Aerwyn rolled over, propped her head on her elbow and confided in her friend in a lowered voice so that Fenn would not overhear, "I know! Coventina kept telling me to think of this as an adventure. Which I stupidly repeated in front of grumpy fins over here" she gestured at Fenn "But I could tell that she was sad and even kind of worried that I was leaving." Now that Aerwyn was thinking deeply about it--which always took her a while to start doing on any subject, usually after she had already taken action--why did she just agree to do this? Why did Coventina ignore all of her embarrassing crying? A magic spell? To make contact with the humans? She understood the need for sure. Her instructors at the Academy had talked to no end about how their race was dying, but how had she gotten mixed up in this seemingly grand task? She rolled over on her back. She had been so quick to just agree and go, even though she was filled with fear. Why did she do things like that? She wondered. Everything was moving so fast.

Folander and Figgs had managed to catch a small cod and were holding it between them when they arrive back at the camp. They sliced it into nine equal pieces, and the mers all sat in their hammocks to enjoy the fresh meat, tearing it in small pieces from the bone. Lachlan had also grabbed some sea berry mush, and they supplemented the meat with a bowl of the juicy fruit stew. Aerwyn was starving, unused to the long slog of swimming for eight hours in one day. The camp was pretty quiet as they all sat around, munching on their dinner, after until Figgs asked Lachlan nonchalantly, "So, how'd you get here anyway?"

"By going on the lam" replied Lachlan.

Chapter 5: The Pacificanans' Story

Lachlan launched into the tale of how the Pacificanas made it to Atlantica. The Pacifica Ocean seat is nestled in a city full of magnificent palaces of sand and stone at the edge of the Hawaiian Mountains, between the Murray and Molokai fracture zones. It had almost double the population of Atlantica. Lachlan, like the rest of the mers from the group, had never left Pacificana, and he had only ever left the city walls when he started his comber training, and, even then, only travelling as far as the west coast of the Americas and east coast of Asia. Since he had been a comber for several years, this put him a few years ahead of Aerwyn in age.

Lachlan described the sand structures within the capitol's city walls with such detail that Aerwyn could almost see the tall, elegant towers, covered in bright bursts of sea anemones, mers bustling about on their day-to-day business, flitting in and out of the tall homes and businesses. Like Atlantica, Pacificana survived mainly on a barter system. Lachlan described how he was raised by just his father, a marlin farmer. He was all set to go into the marlin farming business with his father when he was persuaded by one of his school instructors to become a comber. He promised his father that he would come back to the farming once he grew sick of combing. This had yet to happen, and his father had passed the business down to his little brother. "Oy," he exclaimed, "what a boring life for that wee chap. I wouldn't wish that dull farming nonsense on anyone."

As Lachlan described it, he had never really cared too much about the state of affairs of the kingdom, instead seeking out adventure, warding off sharks, and spending time with his comber friends. It wasn't until about a year ago that he was unable to ignore the reality of the situation any longer. "You see," he told the group, now huddled even closer as the light faded up and out of the waters, "living between two shelves makes it difficult to ignore reality for too long." The fracture zones had become more and more active over the recent years, causing small quakes to reverberate through the ocean every few months or so. Eventually, the quakes came more frequently and stronger, and one quake even toppled several sand towers that had stood for hundreds of years. The most recent structure to topple had been Lachlan's comber academy. Interest piqued, Lachlan started looking into the fracture zone and whether there could be any role for combers in preventing the quakes. While researching the best way to protect his clan from such danger, Lachlan had met Fenn.

As Lachlan described it, they did not become friends immediately. Fenn, the son of Queen Puk Puk and second in line for the throne after his sister Puakai, was not excited about anyone interfering with the royal family. He was on his way to becoming an expert in fracture zones, and had done several years of intense study following his graduation from the academy. Lachlan noted that Fenn made it clear that he really didn't want to work with Lachlan and the combers, and kept him at arms-length for some time.

It became apparent to Lachlan after a few months of trying to persuade Fenn to work with him why he received an initially chilly reception from Fenn. With a kind look and nod at his friend, Lachlan described how Queen Puk Puk had not seemed herself the past year or so and was becoming quite erratic in her behavior. Fenn at first did not allow anyone to get close to her, so they would not be able to see her slowly unravelling, while he tried to figure out how to protect his family and his tribe. At this, Fenn reached over and grabbed Puakai's hand, but he did not look up. His eyes stayed focused on the little red sea anemone opening and closing in front of him. Unfortunately, Lachlan related, her advisors had become close with her as well, and they worked vigorously to push Fenn away and turn Puk Puk against him.

Fenn's royal tutor, the mermagician Earendil, had also tried the ear of Queen Puk Puk about the potential danger of living so close to a fracture zone, but his polite attempts went unheeded. Lachlan described how, before just recently, Earendil had been one of the Queen's trusted advisors for years. She had readily listened to his counsel and tried to govern the clan the best she could. However, after the death of her third child as an infant by heat poisoning about two years ago, she started to lose her connection with the outside world. She would shut herself in her room for days on end, not speaking to another mer, and ordering large amounts of scavenger brandy. At this point, Fenn interrupted "this part isn't important." "Sorry mate," Lachlan replied, "I'll get back on point."

It appeared to Lachlan that, as they tried to reason with Queen Puk Puk about the state of affairs in their sea, they were getting nowhere. There had been a scarcity of food over the last decade or so, but now they were in a full blown famine. It was at this point, when the first recorded death by starvation occurred, that Earendil presented to Fenn his idea about how communication with the humans, to ask them to cut back on harvesting the mers' food and polluting their waters, might be the only solution if they wanted to survive. He disclosed that he had been researching the Eldoris, and that they might be the way to reverse the spell that prevents the mers from having contact with those on the land. Fenn could see some merit in this idea and, upon Earendil's advice, brought it to his mother before he presented it to her panel of advisors. Instead of seeing reason in the plan, which included bringing the heir to the throne, and her only surviving daughter, to far away tribes and the deep seas, she flat out refused. Fenn brought in Earendil to reason with her, and, enraged, she ordered that Earendil be thrown in the dark cells saved for thieves. This crossed the line for Fenn, and he finally decided to engage Lachlan's and the combers' assistance.

From his cell, Earendil coordinated with Lachlan and Fenn to assemble a group to leave Pacificana to unite the Eldoris, without permission from Queen Puk Puk. All in all, they could only gather 18 mers who wanted to take on the task of betraying their queen and travelling to faraway, unknown tribes. Lachlan described how, in the end, he had to persuade Fenn to also go on this journey as well. Fenn wanted the combers to bring the Eldoris to Pacificana, while he waited back with Puakai. Like his mother, Fenn was protective of his little sister. But unlike his mother, he understood the state of affairs of his home. Lachlan described a man torn. It wasn't until Puakai, who had been apprised of the of the plan by Earendil, approached Fenn regarding her desire to go, and that she would go with or without him, that he consented to go. Aerwyn looked at Fenn, still looking at the sea anemone, and then at Earendil. No wonder she sensed some tension between the two of them.

So, it was that in the middle of the night sometime last winter that Earendil was broken out of his cell to lead this journey to unite the Eldoris. The journey had not gone well for the clan members. Of the 18 who had commenced the trip, only five had made it all of the way to Atlantica. First, they were pursued by Queen Puk Puk's finsmen, and ten were captured when the finsmen caught up with the group after just one week.

The five now present, and a few others, had been given enough time by their comrades who sacrificed themselves to escape from the finsmen. Lachlan described Akemi's genius idea that had allowed them to escape. There had been a flotilla of sea turtles migrating above them for several days, moving with the same easy current the mers were on. Akemi's quick thinking had the mers swimming up to the migrating turtles and grasping on to their shells. They splayed their arms and tails on the shells, completely hidden from anyone below looking up. Lachlan laughed when he said that the turtles could not give a care that they were up there. They had ridden on those turtles for several days before they decided that they had not been followed by the finsmen. All of the Pacificanas nodded in agreement when Lachlan made a toast to Akemi and the turtles.

The next hazard that the group faced was the Panama Canal. It was the quickest way from the Pacific Ocean to the Atlantic Ocean. Although undiscoverable by humans, the mers were not immune to the human's industrial aggression. They had waited for the perfect opportunity to cross. They followed a ship navigating the locks, moving from open lock to open lock. The Pacificanans lost a comrade when she was not fast enough getting through the passageway. The lock closed behind the group without warning, and their comrade was crushed in the metal gates. The group lost two other mers, who were crushed between the ship and the side of the Canal.

Once they made it through the Canal, the Pacificanas had a serious discussion about turning back, but Earendil and Puakai insisted on moving forward. Puakai was the highest in command, and no matter how much Fenn had reasoned with her, she would not consent to turn around. She ordered them onward. The rest of the trip to the City of Biscay was marked by a scarcity of fish and other wildlife in the cold waters of the Atlantic, culminating in arriving at the capitol close to starvation.

All of the mers were silent after Lachlan had finished. Aerwyn had not even thought that there had been more of them at the beginning of the trip. A wave of weight seemed to wash over her as she grasped the reality of the situation. It settled down on her body like a giant flat stone. She might die on this task to save their ocean. She shivered, with both excitement and fear and tried to start setting her mind to the task. The anxiety in her belly tried to rear its head.

Chapter 6: A Dropped Eldoris

Aerwyn woke up feeling incredibly sore. She had swum long distances before, but she hadn't ever had to swim all day. Her whole body, from the tips of her fins to her fingernails hurt, and she could feel every single muscle in her body. She also awoke with the distinct feeling of being attracted to Lachlan. Did she have a dream about him? Was it his story from last night? Was it because she had never seen someone with yellow hair before? Was it that he had an openness about him that she recognized in herself? She couldn't tell. But as she lay rolled up in her hammock, she could not help but look over at his, now empty as he had awoken early to relieve Figgs from guarding the camp. Aerwyn rolled over to ask Ula if she was crazy for getting a crush in the middle of a so-called quest, but Ula was gone from her hammock as well. In fact, Aerwyn was the last one to awake. Great, she thought, as she looked at the bustle of preparations around her, this was a fine first impression.

The second morning of their trip to the Arctic started much like the first. They had packed up the giant conch shells with their hammocks and food, strapped in the sea horses, and were on their way through the rocky path of the coastal zone. The light just was filtering through the ceiling of water when

Aerwyn pulled her vest on over her pale green fish scale shirt. Out of the corner of her eye, she could see the mermagician Earendil staring at her intently. She turned her back to him as she laced up her vest, lightly fondling the little iridescent coral hanging from her necklace at the top of the laces. Did he suspect something? She wondered. Or was it again her unique purple skin that had attracted his stare? She shuddered a tiny bit as she placed her silver circlet on her head to hold back her braided hair.

As they started moving, Aerwyn found Ula chatting with Puakai. Both mers had the more traditional circlet of royalty. Ula's included several spikes of coral, with pearls, tiny shells, and other treasures built up on tiny spikes around the circlet, and it was a beautiful rainbow of colors. Aerwyn had always loved this headpiece and had convinced Ula to let her try it on several times. It wasn't much heavier than her simple silver band. Puakai's was made purely of white starfish, and was as delicate as the little mer. Lachlan had asked the prior morning whether it was wise to have the two princesses wear the traditional royal headpieces, thinking it might attract attention to their mission before they wanted it. Earendil had assured him that it would in fact add legitimacy to their small band,

and they wouldn't be mistaken for the roving shipwreck scavengers that lived in the outskirts of the tribes.

Since Ula and Puakai seemed to be bonding over the woes of being princesses, Aerwyn backed off and looked around for someone else to swim with, but everyone seemed to be paired up with someone to talk to. Lachlan's story had put the Atlanticans at ease, and the mers were trying to get used to each other. Looking at Ula and her new friend, the ball of anxiety in Aerwyn's stomach felt like it was glowing a little with loneliness, but she pushed that down and looked around at the beauty around her. They were travelling near the ocean floor again today, as that was the safest way. The path they were on winded through a rocky floor, covered with corals of various colors. They swam through columns of white tubes shooting up from rocks and tall coral trees with spindly pink spikes coming out from all directions. The path was tight at times, and they could not see far in front of them. They met with more wildlife this day, and Aerwyn even saw creepy moray eels rescind back in their rocky homes as they approached. Overhead there were schools of passing fish, who paid the strangers in their waters no mind, briskly going on their ways.

Aerwyn eventually fell to the back of the pack, where Lachlan was leading the sea horses and their heavy burdens. She sidled up to him, saying the first thing she could think of: "so, what is marlin farming like?"

He turned and gave her that wide smile, "boring." She felt shut down with that one word answer, and turned her head to look at the passing scenery. He must have sensed her discomfort, for he followed up with "want to hear about it?"

She smiled, "yeah, I do. We don't have fish farms in Atlantica. Queen Ulayn is very… humane."

"Well, the farms aren't too inhumane," he replied, not a bit offended. "But it is a bunch of the same every day. We keep 'em corralled in a giant floating net. We have to feed 'em every day… move the net to clearer waters, and protect 'em from the bigger fish."

Aerwyn nodded along.

"Then, when they're grown. We harvest them…"

"by…"

"By spearing them and pulling them to edge of the net. The most exciting job is trying to get them through the net without the other fish escaping."

"Oh," Aerwyn replied, "that does sound boring."

"What about you?" Lachlan asked. "What do you do at your home?"

"Well, I'm still at the Academy. I have a year left," she replied, "I don't really know what I want to do next. I kinda wanted to get into human studies... but I also am enjoying this trip so far... so maybe combing?"

"That's cool. I bet you would be good at both," he said, smiling at her.

Aerwyn felt a swirl of water by her side. It was Fenn.

"Lachlan, do you mind, Earendil wants to talk to you about our next stop," Fenn interjected hastily.

"Sure mate," Lachlan turned, "I'll be back. Do you want to lead the horses for a bit Aer?" he said, picking up on Ula's nickname for her.

"Of course," Aerwyn replied, trying to sound confident. Lachlan swam to the front of the group. Fenn had awkwardly remained by her side. Had he heard Lachlan express his confidence in her? If he did, he wasn't showing it.

"So...." Said Aerwyn, "I'm Aerwyn..."

"Yeah" Fenn replied, looking over his shoulder at the shells bobbing along behind them. "Your grandmer is Atlantica's head mermagician."

"Yeah she is" she answered. There was a long silence. Aerwyn felt desperate to fill it, so she said, in an attempt to clear the water, "You know, I know you didn't want me to join... but I promise I won't be a dead weight."

Fenn raised his eyebrows. "We'll see" he responded, and then after a pause, "I need to speak with Earendil." And then he left after again looking over his shoulder, as if to make sure she wasn't going to let the sea horses loose.

They took a break for lunch in a sandy circle, surrounded by pink and white corals. Aerwyn rested her fins on a scooped rock, reclining next to Ula and Puakai, taking in the beauty of her new surroundings. Aerwyn wondered why so many mers moved to gloomy cliffs Biscay when this was just a few days swim away. Lachlan settled down next to her and started regaling all three mermaids with the exciting wildlife that they could meet on this trip. Aerwyn laughed along with his frightening description of the hammerhead shark, but Ula interrupted the story with a reprimand: "you're frightening Princess Puakai Lachlan, try to use some forethought." She put her arm around Puakai and rubbed her shoulder in an act of warmth rare to her. Lachlan looked sheepish and apologized. Ula accepted the apology with a cold smile, and Lachlan snuck a wink to Aerwyn. Aerwyn could feel her face turn a deep shade of purple with pleasure.

Aerwyn spent the rest of the day in the back of the train talking away with Lachlan. He told her about his childhood working on a marlin farm and his life as a comber, and she told him about what it was like having a mermagician for a grandmother. When they stopped for the evening, Aerwyn was physically exhausted, but invigorated by her new friendship.

The next three days were uneventful and tiring, as they traveled along the sandy path surrounded by rocks and corals. Aerwyn found her friendship with Lachlan growing, and was more comfortable around him as she helped him with the horses. She also found that Ula was becoming more and more quiet, and more likely to be found with Puakai than herself. Aerwyn wondered at this, but thought it must be the stress of the journey. There was a nagging feeling pulling at her that maybe she had done something herself to make Ula be more distant. She quietly and tentatively asked Ula about this one evening when they were lying in their hammocks, staring up at the dark currents overhead. Ula had reassured her that she was not mad at Aerwyn and was just nervous about being so far away from Atlantica.

"Do you think that when humans travel over land they have to worry about things like sharks?" Aerwyn then asked, trying to cheer her friend.

"Um probably," Ula replied.

Aerwyn thought of Robin Hood, and what life was like for him in the forest. "It would be really interesting to see what bears are like" she said, almost to herself.

"Right?!" whispered Ula, as the other mers' whispering started to settle down. "What would it be like to be covered in hair like that? So weird."

"Or legs," Aerwyn laughed.

Ula giggled. "Can you imagine having a second set of arms down where our fins are?" Both mers snickered. This wasn't the first time they had imagined their lives as humans.

"Quiet now," bellowed Earendil from somewhere in the darkness, "we need rest for tomorrow." Ula rolled her eyes so dramatically that Aerwyn could see them in the dark. They silently covered their giggles and settled in.

On the fifth day of the journey, Aerwyn finally felt that she was getting in the groove of swimming all day and camping out at night. Then the scenery changed. The difference was so drastic that the whole troupe stopped in their tracks. The rocky sides of the trail ended, and a wall of long green kelp blocked their way. Lachlan halted the horses, and Earendil instructed the group to take a rest as they figured out how to navigate the forest of kelp. Lachlan muscled his way through the curtain of kelp in front of them, and was quickly lost from sight. Figgs and Folander loaded their bows and started the long ascent to the tops of the kelp, going up and up and up until they were small specks in the distance. Aerwyn settled in next to Ula and Puakai, snacking on a small fish cake, watching the action around her. Akemi flitted her tail nervously as she swam to and fro past the seated mers. Fenn and Earendil were in a heated discussion a few fins away. Aerwyn couldn't hear what the two mers were frantically discussing, but Fenn was shaking his head and storming a short way from Earendil before briskly returning with a face so red that it matched his hair. Aerwyn turned to point this out to Ula, who was staring intently at the kelp wall in front of them.

When Fenn swam back to the group he looked even more sullen and withdrawn than he had previously. He sat down by himself, vigorously sharpening a spearhead, which already looked so sharp that it might break off. It took almost an hour before Folander and Figgs returned. "It's way too far up" Figgs said as he simultaneously reached for a jellied fish cake. "We made it a half a league up… maybe one league from the surface--I could actually see things floating up there. But Folander," he said with a mouthful and motioning to his brother, "he almost got stuck in the barrier between us and the land. It was like he was swimming up still, but in slow motion and not going anywhere. It took me a sec to figure out what was going on before I could pull him out of it and back down to me." Figgs grabbed another fish cake, "I don't think that way is going to work mates. We can't make it high enough to swim over the kelp. And we couldn't see over the kelp to see how far the forest extends." His brother nodded along, clearly exhausted from his struggle in the barrier.

Soon, Lachlan joined them. His jolly face poked out from the curtain of kelp, looking as upbeat as usual. "Looks good this way," he stated, as he tried pulling the kelp pieces stuck to the human part of his body off. Ula left her seat on the mossy rock to help him. Aerwyn thought he was blushing a little as she worked on his back. "You can't see much in there, but I saw no evidence of any predators. I went about thirty minutes before I headed back, and there was no letting up on the kelp. What about you guys?" Figgs and Folander filled him in on their scouting trip. "Perhaps we should start out tomorrow morning, in case the forest is large and it takes us a day to get through it?" Lachlan suggested.

"No" replied Earendil, speaking up for the first time since the combers had returned. "We already travel too slow. It is only midday--we must push through rather than lose half of a day." Lachlan shrugged good naturedly, and Figgs looked at Folander a bit reluctantly. His brother insisted "I'm fine mate. Just stop hogging all of those cakes and let me nourish myself a bit." The combers handed the defensive spears to everyone this time, and they set off.

Traveling through the kelp forest was slower going than Aerwyn had initially thought upon seeing it. The strands were thick and strong, and had to be pushed aside enough so that the seahorses and shells could fit through. She could see why the experienced travelers of the group had been nervous about entering the forest. You could barely see ahead of you, and you had no idea what was lurking to your left your right. It was beautiful though, thought Aerwyn. It was darker in the forest, since much sunlight was blocked out from the kelp. It reminded Aerwyn of the human stories she had read about humans using fire lanterns to make their way through dense trees. Eventually, they did have to bring out the angler fish in a cage that they had packed for the trip. Although mers were more accustomed to dark places than humans were, they still could not see well in the complete dark. The water around the tall slippery strands filtered its colors and was almost caramel colored inside the forest.

No one was talking very much. It was eerily beautiful in the caramel and green hazy forest, and no one wanted to be the mer to attract anything that could be lurking amongst the strands. At one point, they heard a rustling in the kelp off to the left of the party. At the signal of Lachlan, all of the mers stayed perfectly still for several minutes, ears perked to the sound. But the whatever is was never came back. They travelled on and on through the dense forest, and it became harder and harder to see forward as daylight from above was quickly running out. Aerwyn thought they must have been swimming in this forest for near six hours. Ula was in front of her and Aerwyn could tell she was tiring out. Never as strong of a distance swimmer as Aerwyn, being much smaller and slender and a better sprinter, she was having as much difficulty as the little Puakai in keeping pace. Aerwyn was about to reach a reassuring hand on her friend's shoulder when a sickening electric pain encircled her tail like a razor.

All at once, panic set in the little group. Aerwyn looked down to see what was on her tail and saw the mold less form of a clear jelly fish seeking to attach itself to her tail. "Arrrrghhhh!" She yelled "Get off of me you beast!" She

69

swung the spear at it, swatting at it instead of stabbing it. As she struggled with its form, heaving her tail this way and that to prevent it from sticking its neon strings into her scales again, she heard the others about her going about the same struggle. The pain of where she had been stung was searing and rage inducing. She slashed madly at the slimy form, attempting to end its attempts. Another string slashed at her. This time the pain came from her torso. Her panic turned to fear as she recalled that the jelly fish sought the heart of its victims to cease its struggle before consuming its prey in its wide, yellowed, stringy mouth. She jabbed at it again, this time, piercing the bubble with the point of her spear. Again, she hit it. And again. She became aware someone else fending it off, and between the two of them, the jelly fish had had enough. It slunk back into the screen of kelp. Aerwyn could see that the other jelly fish were doing the same thing, creeping back into the protection of the kelp. She looked over at her helper, Fenn, for just long enough to give him a grateful smile. He actually smiled back with a mixture of relief and adrenaline. "Swim as fast as you can out of here!" Yelled Earendil. "Those were the scouts, they will be going back to get the rest of the bloom after us!" The short, shared smile ended and Aerwyn and Fenn started swimming frantically with the rest of the group.

As she swam, she sensed something was off. "My necklace!" Thought Aerwyn aloud. "It must have come off in the struggle. I must go back for it!"

Fenn, who was swimming hard next to her replied "let it go! We can't fend off a whole bloom together."

"I can't" cried Aerwyn, thinking of the Eldoris hanging from it. "I must go back."

"Don't!" Yelled Fenn as Aerwyn turned around.

"Go on without me" she retorted.

The rest of the group swam on, Ula looking worriedly back at her. Soon, they were out of sight as Aerwyn frantically searched the sea floor for the iridescent coral. Fenn, torn on whether to go or stay, decided on hanging several fins away. It was hard to see in the dimming evening light, but after what seemed hours, that were in fact just a few minutes, Aerwyn saw the necklace half buried in sand on the ground. She swooped down to grab it. As her hand closed around it and she came back upright, she found herself eye to eye with at least a hundred clear jelly fish, hovering in the protection of the kelp. The bloom had returned for its dinner. "Swim!" she heard Fenn cry in the distance. She shoved the necklace in her satchel and took off in his direction. He waited for her to catch up with him, postured with his bow and sending little darts into the bloom of predators approaching. When she reached him, he swung his bow on his back and struck out after her.

They swam for what seemed like hours. By the time they reached the edge of the kelp forest, they could barely see the others in the distance through the dark waters, their angler fish lighting the way. When they caught up with the others, finally finding the safety in numbers again, Fenn rounded on Aerwyn as she bent over, trying to catch her breath.

"What were you thinking!?" he barked. The look on his face contorted the handsome features into the face of a stern schoolmaster. "You put us all at risk, you put this mission at risk, for a piece of jewelry! A lousy, stinking piece of jewelry! You could have died in that bloom. I could have died."

Aerwyn, still trying to catch her breath, unbent her body and met his furious eyes with her own and could think of nothing to say. His blue eyes had no ounce of understanding in them. She felt terrible about dropping the necklace, and she knew she had put them at risk by going back for it. But she also knew that she had to go back for it--that she had no choice. But she could not say that to the group, all now looking at her with questioning eyes. She could not give away that she, not Ula, held the Eldoris. Ula's life, Figgs' and Folander's lives, and hers, might depend on it at some point.

Forcing herself to say something, anything, she gushed out, still gasping for breath, "I'm sorry, I wasn't thinking."

"You weren't thinking? You weren't thinking? We can't afford mers who don't think on this mission!" Fenn retorted.

"I'm sorry Fenn" Aerwyn pleaded. "I'm sorry everyone" she said to her companions, beseeching them to forgive her with her eyes.

Ula was the first one to respond, "just don't do it again Aerwyn." Lachlan gave her an encouraging smile, and Figgs and Folander shrugged their shoulders to let her know they were over it already. Akemi and Puakai smiled embarrassed for her, but didn't say anything.

Earendil broke the awkward silence by saying: "Okay everyone. I think we learned a lot today. This journey to Arcticana is going to be more dangerous than a jaunt outside the city walls. We need to be more vigilant in our scouting and guarding. Let's make camp for the night and be on our way tomorrow. Fenn, you need to cool off--you've got first watch." Fenn stormed off without a word.

They set up their hammocks inside a small cave they found near the edge of the kelp forest. It was very small, and their beds would be touching during the night, but no one had complaints about not sleeping in the open that night. They all gathered around a little geyser at the mouth of the cave. It was comforting and reminded the mers of the quiet murmur of the geysers in their dwellings back home. They all sat quietly in a circle, munching on their dinner of jellied clams and dulse, mending spears that were broken during the attack, putting sardine oil on the tender sting lines on their fins and torsos, and making little conversation. Aerwyn attempted to discreetly mend the necklace, and succeeded in getting all of the coral beads back on the string. She motioned to Ula, who shifted in her seat to tie it around her neck.

"Can you double knot it Ula? It wasn't tight enough last time."

Ula rested her hand on Aerwyn's shoulder, "I know." She said it kindly. Did she know about the Eldoris, Aerwyn thought? Or was she being annoyingly condescending? Aerwyn squeezed her arm, and Ula squeezed back.

As Aerwyn settled into her hammock, exhausted from the day, but unable to sleep, she thought about Fenn. He had risked his life staying back and waiting for her. If he hated her so much, why would he do that? Was he just an honorable mer? Oh well, Aerwyn told her sleepy mind, it doesn't matter now. If he didn't hate her before, he certainly does now.

Chapter 7: Hotel de la Queen Victoria

The small cave was warm with the geyser water when the mers awoke. No one wanted to move for a long time, and they all lay together in the cave in silence, the sting lines on their bodies now just a dull throb. Aerwyn felt Ula's fins resting on top of her fins, and she could feel Akemi breathing on the other side, the small bubbles from her gills gently bumping into the side of her face. For the first time since they had left Atlantica a week ago, Aerwyn felt a part of something. She thought, because the other mers were also resting and enjoying the calm together, they must be feeling it as well. Aerwyn studied the cave ceiling, with the green moldy stalactites hanging down. It reminded her of Ula's bedroom in the palace, but adorned with natural formations instead of the hanging beads.

Earendil interrupted this silence by entering the cave-- apparently he had woken earlier. No wonder we were all relaxed, thought Aerwyn, the old grump wasn't around. "Let's get up everyone" Earendil barked. "We can't waste the day lounging in this cave--we still have several weeks ahead of us, and the sooner we get on the course the better."

As soon as she moved her body, Aerwyn was wracked with pain. According to the sounds the other mers made as they stirred, she knew she must not be alone. What had been a dull throbbing in the two places she had been stung, turned into an electric pain that moved in sharp, knife-like waves through her body. Earendil, who was the only mer who had not taken a sting, looked at the group of writhing mers, crying out in pain in the cave with disappointment.

"Where in the sea could we be going like this," asked Folander, who was cradling his arm.

"Not far," responded Earendil. "We will travel a short distance and spend the rest of the day and tomorrow resting. There is not much I can do besides keep administering my sardine oil. You all need to rest. Movement is what causes the poison to spread. But I am fearful that this cave does not have enough protection from that bloom of jellyfish. If they sense our weakness, they will come back."

The mers struggled to pack up the camp. Every twist of her tail made Aerwyn draw a sharp intake of water through her gills. But Earendil pressed them to get going. They were moving uphill closer to the coastline than the day before. Aerwyn thought this had to do for safety reasons, since the deep seas often held the largest predators. But, in all of the sea weeds and coral around her, she could not see far enough up to know orient herself as to their depth.

Puakai was in too much pain to move, and had been harnessed into a conch shell, which was moving slowly behind the group as the seahorses struggled with their extra burden. The rest were swimming along at an excruciatingly slow pace. Earendil himself had his shoulder under Ula, dragging her along. Aerwyn was tired, in terrible pain, and emotionally depleted. She thought about swimming up to where Fenn was silently moving along, to apologize again for the day before. But his rigid shoulders, and lack of eye contact all morning, had made her feel like it was a useless cause. She stared at the long, swollen welt on his back. With every flick of his tail his back muscles contracted, causing him to flinch in pain from the wound. She wanted more than anything to thank him for helping her. But, she didn't know what to say that she hadn't already said. She thought about revealing the real Eldoris to him, but remembered Coventina's warning to trust no one. She would have to be comfortable with him being mad at her. She knew that was an impossible task for her.

The mers struggled on for only about an hour before they reached their destination. They stopped on a ridge that overlooked a sandy valley. It was easy to see in the distance, looming up like a colossal boulder. Aerwyn had never seen anything like it before in her life. It was a sunken human ship, upside down in the sand. In front was a sign that read "Hotel de la Queen Victoria." The first mers that Aerwyn and the band had seen in a week were specks in the distance, swimming into the hotel.

"How wonderful!" Puakai clapped her hands from her seat in the conch shell. "I've heard of hotels such as these! My mother told me about the Grand Titanic Hotel and how all of the ladies and gentlemers used to travel there on holidays, feasting and dancing the night away."

Earendil put his hand on Puakai's shoulder. "Times are different now Princess. These hotels have become havens for the rouge wanderers and scavengers. Since the tribes stopped prioritizing the connectivity of the oceans, relics of the old days such as this hotel are no longer safe holiday destinations for global travelers. Everyone," he said, turning to the rest of the group. "I want you to all be vigorous in looking out for each other. Assume every mer you meet is out for her or himself. Tell no one what we are doing here. Our story is that we are on guided tour of the Atlantic, by me, and that you are merely vacationers who ran into some trouble with jellyfish." Aerwyn stole a peep at Fenn when Earendil said the vacation part, but he remained expressionless. "Keep to yourselves. And princesses, remove your crowns." And, with that eerie warning, the mers made their way down the ridge and across the sandy valley to the shipwreck hotel.

The hotel was massive. When Aerwyn looked up at it from the entrance, she could see at least four stories above her. The entrance, once a gilded and intricately carved coral door frame built in between the masts of the ship, was covered in barnacles and weeds, in desperate need of some upkeep. The clerk's desk was nestled in the sand, with the massive deck of the ship hanging overhead. The desk was empty, and Earendil moved ahead of the group to ring the bell that had a human sign next to it that said "Please ring for service." It felt right out of a human novel.

A little old merman came hustling out from behind a sandy mound behind the desk. He seemed very pleased to have so many visitors, and fussed over which rooms to give his distinguished guests. "Well, well, because the Queen Victoria has made her bed upside down, the best rooms, with the views you know, you can see the Atlantic Mountains in the background! Those rooms, they are pretty small. The ones on the first floor are the best! But you might be apt to find a fish or two. I try to keep 'em out, but it's just me on most days up here. We do have a staff… because I mean, we do get some passersby, and they need to eat! I can't cook. That's why I keep this job, for the sustenance you know. The owner, he doesn't come around much anymore. Seems to me he lost the desire to travel, just like all the mers. But you are travelling! How wonderful! Where are you headed my merfolk?!"

Earendil impatiently retorted to the rambling mer, "Four two hammock rooms and one one hammock room please. I don't care where they are at."

Once rooms were assigned, Lachlan swam back out through the entrance to stable the seahorses in the hotel's stables near the bow ship. The rest of the mers followed the clerk into the hotel through an opening in the ceiling, spiraling through the staircase to the second floor. The clerk had apparently decided to provide them with the larger but less scenic rooms after Earendil's briskness. "I've put you here, rooms 301 to 305. Here are your keys. Dinner will be in the ballroom on the fourth floor, which is actually the first floor since we are upside down you know. If you are inclined to check out the view," he looked hesitantly at Earendil, as if he hoped he wouldn't get interrupted by him again, "you can take that staircase we were on there up to the first floor. There is a hatch up there. We keep it open all the time. There's a net though. The net keeps the fishes out. We still get some fishes in here though. Sorry 'bout that. But you can go up there and lounge on the bottom of the boat and see for leagues." With that he gave the room keys, old rusty skeleton keys, to Earendil, and headed back down the staircase.

Earendil handed a key to Ula, Puakai, and Figgs. Aerwyn quickly grabbed the key from her friend. It was an amazing human relic. To be holding one thrilled Aerwyn to the bone. She tucked it into her vest pocket, returning her hand there to slide her fingers on the rusty metal every few minutes. Even though it was still just late morning, when Aerwyn threw herself on her hammock in her room, she fell asleep immediately. The pain all over her body was intense, and it was wearing her out. As she closed her eyes, she felt happy not to move, and happy to be out of the wild of the ocean.

When Aerwyn awoke, the fingers of daylight through the window were thinning. She looked down and saw Ula had also slept through the day and, as her gaping mouth made apparent, was still knocked out. Aerwyn sat up in her hammock and looked around. The room was very large. The mers' hammocks were spacious and covered in cushions woven from seaweed silk. The hammocks were strung like bunks where Aerwyn suspected the human beds had once been. Because the boat had landed upside down, the room's extravagant, but now dulled, crystal chandelier posed as centerpiece to the room. A piece of glass had been laid upon it, with little glass chairs all around it. It made a quaint and beautiful table. The hotel owner had preserved the oil paintings, and turned them 180 degrees, so that guests wouldn't have to swim upside down to admire them. Everything was covered in gel growth and seaweed--as if it was too much for the one clerk to come in and polish it away. These growths were not what Aerwyn had expected, and it gave the room a bit of a creepy feel. The window was pretty useless-- it was covered with a net to keep the fish out, but was so close to the ground that Aerwyn had to lay on the ground to see out of it.

This struggle woke Ula up, who snorted with laughter at her friend rolling on the ground. "Ha! What are you doing Aerwyn!? Ugh" as her laugh made her stings surge with pain.

"I'm just checking out this spectacular view." Said Aerwyn looking up with a grin.

The mers decided they should probably go check out the view at the bottom of the boat, just so that they wouldn't have to hurt the clerk's feelings the next time they saw him, because he would, without a doubt, ask them if they had seen it. They wandered down the eerily quiet hall and up into the stairwell hole. They swam up three flights, into the well of the boat, where they saw a bronze plated sign that said "guests welcome" near a netted opening. They pulled the net to the side and popped their heads out. No one else was up there. There were scattered chairs and hammocks strewn about, and a potted sea anemone here and there. The hull seemed well tended to, and Aerwyn could see why the clerk might find this the best part of the otherwise depressing hotel. The view was phenomenal. Aerwyn could see off to the left the forest of kelp that they had come from. It was a fuzzy green mass, lit from the top by the fading sunlight. She could also see in the far distance to the right the looming shapes of the Atlantic mountain range. She shivered with relief that they didn't have to cross those. All she really remembered about them from her studies was that they teemed with the large and brutal sea predators.

Aerwyn and Ula rested on the hull, taking in the view, until it got dark. Little fish were swimming overhead, and it was peacefully quiet. This was the first time that they had been alone since the start of the trip. They talked about the library, Ula's mom, and Coventina. For the first time in a week, Aerwyn felt like herself. She felt normal and close to her friend. It was like they were on a vacation, rather than on a quest. Just as the last light was fading from the sea, Ula's stomach made a loud gurgling sound. The mers laughed at it and realized that they had slept through their midday meal. They agreed they should go down to the fourth floor to check out the dining room. They struggled down the stairway with their aching bodies, but their spirits were high as their friendship had refreshed their hearts.

Chapter 8: Fast Friends

Before Aerwyn went to the Academy, at age seven, she spent most of her time with Coventina. They had not yet moved into the City of Biscay, and lived in a little cave in the outskirts of the city. They didn't move into the city until Aerwyn started at the Academy and Coventina joined the Queen's council. She and Coventina would spend their days working on their garden, learning lessons to prepare her for the academy, and practicing swimming. Maybe that was why Aerwyn didn't know that she was different from everyone else. She had seen other mers who were green, but her grandmother had rainbow coloring, and Aerwyn thought their differences were normal.

It wasn't until she attended her first Biscay Brine Festival, that Aerwyn sensed she was different. The City was decorated with colorful anemones, gathered in the fields surrounding the City and transplanted to new homes on the stone posts surrounding the city center and amphitheater. The Biscay Brine Festival was a yearly games in which the best of the city would compete in different tasks, such as spear hurtling, sprint swimming, blowfish wrangling, and eel riding. It had taken the place of the Aequorial Games, when the tribes from all five oceans would gather each year for games, policy meetings, and celebratory feasts. The Atlanticans maintained some of the old Five traditions, and they added a few new ones of their own.

She recalled arriving hand in hand with her grandmer. At first, she thought the mers were staring at Coventina. It wasn't until a little mer pointed right at her that she realized that they were looking at her. Never having felt self-conscious before, Aerwyn was very confused by the wave of doubt that flooded over her. To this day she could still feel the visceral reaction. But Coventina ignored the looks and comments, and so Aerwyn did too. She marched up to the start of the junior relay swim sprints race and gave the official her name. The mer was just polite enough to close her gaping mouth before pointing Aerwyn to a group of mers her similar age, lined up in four lines of various sizes. She swam to the closest one. A bigger mermaid shook her head as Aerwyn approached, so Aerwyn headed toward the next line.

"Uh, why are you purple?" Asked a mer a little shorter than her, as she lined up for the race.

"Um… because I am," she answered.

"Well, you can't be in this line… you're too weird looking," the mermaid answered.

"Yeah, we want to win, get in another line" a merboy chimed in.

Aerwyn looked back at Coventina, who was purposefully ignoring the whole interaction. Aerwyn's heart sank. Should she join another line? Go back to Coventina? That was the moment she met Ula. She would never forget that moment. Taller than her then as well, Ula approached from the line one over. "Come into my line" She called, beckoning Aerwyn over. Aerwyn hadn't known she was holding her breath, but her relief was so great that it all came out in a swoosh. She swam over to Ula's line. "Don't worry about them," said the little princess, "let's show them and win this!" And they did. Aerwyn swam faster than she ever had before in her life. She swam away from that feeling of self-consciousness that had started to creep into her former blindly confident self. She swam away from that feeling from that day on, and she tried as hard as she could to never let it catch her. Still, she couldn't help but wonder about her skin at times. Why she was the purple magicless granddaughter to a mermagician, and everyone else got to be just green normal mers with normal expectations laid upon them.

The two friends had been on the winning team every year since that first junior relay race. Ula was a little faster than Aerwyn, and she would beat her in every fin to fin contest. Aerwyn didn't mind being second fastest to her friend--she was used to being second to her in all things. They also were inseparable since that moment. Ula didn't have much patience for anyone but Aerwyn, and sometimes she had no patience for Aerwyn. Aerwyn had found a friend who celebrated differences and, while she didn't ever ignore her purple skin, acted like it was no big deal.

Chapter 9: Scavengers

When Ula and Aerwyn swam into the dining room, they were surprised at how many guests were actually staying at the hotel. They were the last to arrive from their group, and there were four other small groups sitting around various tables. The dining hall, although tired and worn with barnacles sprinkled here and there, was magnificent. The polished chandeliers served as table stands. The glass tabletops enabled the guests to view their sparkling crystals as they tinkled in the water. The art work had all been turned around the right way, and portraits of humans, land creatures, and land vistas surrounded the guests, giving the room an exotic feel. The room was well lit with tiny angler fish, trapped in the room and swimming about freely. They made it feel as if the room was sparkling. Music was coming from a coral pipe player in the corner of the room. Aerwyn looked closer and saw that it was the same clerk from earlier in the day. He caught her looking at him and winked at her. Aerwyn smiled and quickly turned to the group. It was clear that what staff the hotel had left had put all of their efforts into this one room. It was bright and quite like what Aerwyn imagined actual humans had experienced when staying on the ship.

They were seated at a large glass table. The restaurant here operated the same way that the restaurants in Atlantica had. The dishes were served in very heavy pots with lids, so as to keep them from floating away. The mers would scoop their food from the pots with the clamshells provided at their place setting and then eat the food right off of the shell. Aerwyn was surprised the food was so good, considering the lack of staff and wondered where the chef was. They ate squid boiled in a rich green kelp sauce, hundreds of miniature fish cakes, stewed sea grass with spicy sauce of what Aerwyn did not know, and coral cakes of all flavors and colors. Perhaps it had been the lack of a hot meal for over a week, or because she had skipped lunch, but Aerwyn was ravenous and kept refilling her plate. Conversation was light at the table as her companions did the same.

Aerwyn sat beside Lachlan and across from Ula. Lachlan talked to her a lot, making jokes and teasing Aerwyn about how much she was eating. He kept both of the mers quietly laughing throughout the dinner. His impression of Earendil's harsh stare made it hard for them to remain muted, and their table became the most boisterous of the dining room. Even Earendil laughed at Lachlan's impression. Maybe he isn't so grumpy, thought Aerwyn. Fenn seemed to be having a good

91

time too and was also the butt of Lachlan's jokes. Lachlan made him laugh at one point, and Fenn threw back his head, showing a row of perfect white teeth, and to Aerwyn's surprise, a very charming smile.

The group was merry, perhaps because of the relief of being out of the elements, or perhaps because they were all finally becoming comfortable with each other. They were learning about each other's home oceans, and comparing notes about the leadership, food, schooling, and career paths. All except Earendil were pretty young, but everyone besides Aerwyn had a tract they were on or had picked out. Aerwyn listened about the life of a comber, the plight of the farmer, and the woes of a princess as Puakai told funny yet endearing stories about her staff, including Earendil. Eventually, as the evening wore on, the group pushed their plates away and lounged around the table sipping on wakame juice. Everyone, including Earendil, was in good spirits. He was in fact regaling the crowd about his journeys as a young mer. Unlike the rest of the group, he had traveled beyond his own ocean. The angler fish lights were dimming, and the room became more and more peaceful.

Despite her contentedness, Aerwyn could not ignore the fact that they were being watched by the small groups of mers straggling in and out of the dining room. She wondered how many of the travelers were scavengers--lawless mers who lived off the land, traveling from place to place, seeking shelter where they could and eating anyone's food. Earendil had warned them about scavengers, that they could be ruthless and selfish. As far as Aerwyn could tell, the mers at the Queen Victoria seemed weary and haggard, not the threatening warlike roamers she had imagined.

Late in the evening, mer by mer they wandered back to their rooms, groaning with the initial movement of getting up from the table. Earendil handed each a vial with his salve for the stings as they got up. Earendil had decided that they would spend one more day at the hotel resting, since most of the mers were still pretty sore. Finally, Aerwyn and Ula left when Lachlan got up, leaving Fenn and Earendil alone.

Lachlan swam Ula and Aerwyn to their door. When Aerwyn said good night, Lachlan smiled at her and said good night, but he didn't go anywhere. Aerwyn got the distinct impression that Ula and Lachlan were just waiting for her to open the door, so Aerwyn opened it up and went inside, but they didn't follow her. Instead they just floated there, both smiling at her. Unsure what to do she said "errrr" and closed the door. What's that all about, she thought. The peep hole in the door was by the floor, so she lowered herself on her stomach to get a look out. All she could see were their fins, about a foot apart. She put her ear to the door. She could hear some muffled talking, but that was about it. Hmmm, she thought. Was something going on there? Aerwyn sighed. This was a classic Ula. Ula, as a princess, and beautiful at that, always got what she wanted. Aerwyn looked at her purple arms, rotating them side to side. Thanks mom and dad, whoever you are, for this... it's really helping me out. She tried not to cry, but she couldn't help a few tears seeping out from her eyes. It's not even that I like him, she thought to herself, but I thought he liked me.

Aerwyn heard Ula come in the room a few minutes later, but she pretended to be asleep. Her conscience was bothering her. She felt weird about Lachlan. Had she turned him off by tagging along with him at the rear of the group these past few days? Were he and Ula talking about that? Was he trying to get advice about how to let her down? Or, was he trying to get advice about how to make a move? She smiled slightly, that could be it too she thought. She tried to make her mind rest so she could sleep, but as was her way, once she started reliving moments from the day, she couldn't help but think about what she had said at each moment, and wince about how weird she was.

Coventina had told her that she needed to give these worries but a moment to glance at, and then tuck away out of sight forever, because they weren't worth the time and energy to perseverate over. This was difficult for Aerwyn. She cared what people thought of her. As much as she wished she could be like Coventina or Ula or Ulayn, Aerwyn dreaded the thought that someone didn't like her. Hopefully Lachlan at least liked her as a friend. And Fenn, he clearly didn't like her. Maybe I should see if I can set that straight, she thought. Then I can tuck that away. She knew that is not what Coventina meant, she was definitely wasting time and energy on this. But she could not help herself from wanting to resolve this misunderstanding.

Aerwyn rolled out of her hammock and off of her copious soft silk pillows. By Ula's measured breathing, Aerwyn could tell that she was sleeping. She must have been thinking for a long time, because Ula had trouble sleeping usually. Aerwyn crept out of the room and quietly closed the door behind her. She swam down the hall to the stairwell to check to see if Fenn was still in the dining room. As she reached the stairwell, she heard angry voices coming from below. Panicked, not knowing whether it was a scavenger or stranger, Aerwyn tucked into a small opening near the top of the room, which looked like it had once been a closet. The voices moved closer and Aerwyn could make out Fenn and Earendil's distinct Pacificanan accents.

"I don't care" Fenn was saying in a quiet but very strong voice. "If I see that she is not going to make it, I'm pulling her out!"

Earendil, in his calm emotionless, gravelly voice replied "I really don't think it will come to that Fenn, and we shall just worry about it when the time comes."

"You keep saying that!" Fenn retorted. "But, how do I know you're not going to play it out all the way, even if she dies?"

"I'll do what is best for the mers, Fenn. My duty as a mermagician and a dedicated scholar of the oceans is to ensure that we have an ocean to live in."

"You're not giving me a clear answer though" shot Fenn.

"I don't have one" Earendil replied quietly.

The mers glided past Aerwyn's hiding spot. Aerwyn didn't dare to move until she heard two different doors close. What in the world could they be talking about? Was this about the Eldoris? Would collecting the Eldoris kill someone? Was one of the Eldoris in a dangerous spot? Should I tell Ula? Aerwyn was full of curiosity, and a little fearful, as she tucked herself back in bed. No, she thought, as she looked at her friend sleeping, her ever growing worry lines smooth for once. I'll not tell Ula. It will only worry her. She fell into a restless sleep.

The next morning at breakfast, Aerwyn did get a chance to apologize to Fenn. The jellyfish stings had subsided enough that they were now just a dull reminder of the incident. Still, Aerwyn was looking forward to one more day of rest at the hotel, which she was excited to explore. She spotted Fenn by his thick, orange hair and sat next to him, saying in a rush "hey, I just wanted to apologize for putting you at risk. I didn't expect you to wait for me. Thank you for helping me out." Fenn looked taken aback for a second, his hand halfway to his mouth with a spoonful of sweet urchin mush. He blinked, and then his impenetrable expression returned. "Just don't do something like that again." He responded as he finished taking his bite. It wasn't as chilly as Aerwyn expected, and Fenn did engage in conversation with her at breakfast this time, even laughing at one of her jokes about the clerk. His smile was actually pretty cute Aerwyn thought, he had deep dimples and very straight teeth. Maybe we can be friends after all thought Aerwyn.

Ula and Aerwyn spent the day exploring the hotel with Lachlan. The rest of the group split off in twos and threes: Fenn and Puakai spent most of the day on the roof of the hotel,

Figgs and Folander and Akemi left the hotel to explore the surrounding area, and Earendil kept to his room. Aerwyn enjoyed exploring the halls and rooms of the shipwreck, and was excited when she could point out things that she had learned about reading human novels, such as oil lamps and fire hoses.

Despite the fun she was having in the protection of the ship, Aerwyn couldn't help but feel uneasy. Today the scavengers staying at the hotel seemed less inclined to hide their stares, and Aerwyn caught them staring at her on several occasions. One of the scavengers even asked them about their group, as a few of them were sitting down to dinner. The rest of the group had not arrived yet. Not wanting to be rude, Aerwyn smiled and repeated the story that Earendil had told them to tell. "Oh, we are on a guided trip of Atlantica. I'm still in school you know, and I'm trying to learn about my home ocean!" The scavenger just looked at her, expressionless.

Lachlan stepped in, "listen sir, we don't want any trouble. We are just trying to enjoy our trip." The mer didn't say anything, and turned away to go join a couple of other scraggly looking scavengers on the far end of the dining room.

"Yikes" said Ula. "He gives me the creeps."

Once the rest of the group got to dinner, they started to plan out the next step of their trip. At this point, they had been travelling for one week. It would take two more weeks to get to the capitol settlement of Arcticana. They would need to pass through the Norwegian Sea and Greenland Sea on the way. Aerwyn remembered reading about these seas at the academy. They were well known for their deadly sea life and dangerous geography. The plan was to swim through these seas at a fast clip, so as to not dwell in the dangerous waters. As Earendil was softly murmuring these plans, Aerwyn noticed that the scavengers had quietly left the dining room, their food untouched. That's weird she thought. She elbowed Figgs, who was to her left, and nodded her head toward the empty table. Figgs made eye contact with Earendil, who maintained his current expression, and Figgs hopped up and said "I'm going to head out for a bit of air, Folander, do you care join brother?" The two mers left the dining room through the front entrance.

Minutes passed with the group, ticking by slowly. Then, suddenly, Aerwyn heard a commotion coming from the hallway. She looked at Ula, unsure of what to do, while Fenn, Akemi, and Lachlan all flipped up their fins into an upright position. "We know you have it mate--and we don't want any trouble, but I saw it. You have it there under your cloak."

Figgs was saying in a loud voice that sounded friendly with undercurrents of dead seriousness. "Just give it back, and we can all just go on our way." Aerwyn sensed others starting to move towards the door that the sound was coming from, that led to the stairwell to the rooms, and she followed suit. Through the doorway, Aerwyn saw Figgs and Folander eye-to-eye with three scavengers, who each had their hand at his hip, on the handle of what looked like a knife. Aerwyn felt very uneasy grateful in this moment for their numbers, and for the other mers' confidence. As Akemi and Lachlan took their places behind Figgs and Folander, and Earendil and Aerwyn stepped in behind them, they now outnumbered them six to three.

The scavengers looked uncomfortable, and they exchanged a quick glance with each other before the tall one took something from his rotted cloak and threw it to the ground. "We're not done with you yet. We know you've got a mer here that would raise a good ransom. I don't know which one she is," he said eyeing Akemi and Aerwyn, "but you better watch your backs." And with that, the three scavengers turned on their fins, and headed up the stairwell. Aerwyn looked to the ground where the object had been thrown. Lachlan was bending to pick it up. She inhaled sharply. It was Ula's crown.

Ula! She thought, where was she? She turned to swim back to the dining room. Ula was with Fenn and Puakai, talking with the clerk at his place on the stage. Fenn was casually leaning on the stage, and pointing his arm about the room as if he were asking questions about the splendid décor. But Aerwyn could see that the muscles in his jaw were tight and his eyes were sharp and watchful. Ula and Puakai were holding hands. At this moment Aerwyn felt many things. She felt upset with herself that she hadn't thought to ensure her friend was safe before rushing to see what was happening. She felt distant from her friend as she saw her holding Puakai's hand for comfort. She understood what Ula must be feeling, but had tried to joke with her about it to make her feel better. Now Ula now had a serious compatriot who was going through the exact same thing. She also felt admiration for Fenn who had been very quick on his fins.

Fenn swam up next to Aerwyn. She smiled tentatively at him, as if to say thank you for taking care of her friend, and also to show that she was not afraid after the confrontation with the scavengers. He responded by tilting his head close to hers and whispering "We're leaving this place at midnight. It's too dangerous. Please pass the message on to the rest *discreetly*." Aerwyn felt a little annoyed. Of course I will be discreet, she thought. How inept do you think I am? She watched Fenn swim back to his sister and take her hand. Whenever I think I'm proving I'm meant to be here, he makes certain I know I'm not.

Chapter 10: Swimming North

The water was still pitch black when Aerwyn made her way to the meeting place in front of the hotel. By the time she and Ula arrived, Lachlan had already packed up the conch shells and harnessed the seahorses. Earendil was bartering with the clerk for some additional supplies, and Aerwyn saw a packet of coral cakes and was inwardly grateful. As they started out their trek, after a few days of much needed rest, the mers had the squinty eyed look of few hours of sleep and a determination to make it through the day ahead. Aerwyn gingerly touched her torso, luckily, the sting pain had subsided quite a bit.

The Hotel de la Queen Victoria was seated in the North Sea, and it took the mers two unremarkable days to make it through the North Channel, and then two more across the continental shelf, keeping the land mass to their right and the ominous Atlantic Ridge to their left. Once they left the landmass behind, fish and vegetation became more and more sparse. They were deep enough that the sea life of the continental shelf was few and far between, and there was limited life on the sloping rocky and sandy continental slope. They kept the slope to their right for protection, but the open ocean to the left made Aerwyn feel exposed. She also had the uncomfortable feeling of being watched. She kept trying to brush it off as uneasiness due to the different terrain, but she kept looking behind her. There was nothing there but dark waters and a few floating particles. She hung back with Lachlan and the sea horses and tried to distract herself from the nagging feeling in gut.

When they made camp after emerging from the North Sea, Ula was particularly moody. She started setting up her hammock next to Puakai, rather than her usual spot next to Aerwyn. Aerwyn approached her friend and asked "Hey Ula, don't you want to sleep next to me?"

"Sure" Ula replied, not moving her hammock.

After dinner, Ula swam to the exterior of the camp and sat on a large piece of brain coral. Aerwyn followed her. "Hey, are you okay," she asked as she came upon her friend who was fiddling with a hermit crab on the sea floor.

Ula looked up briefly, but then turned back to the crab. "Yeah. I guess so," she replied. She poked at it with her long green finger. It was unhappy at the attention and retreated into his shell.

"You don't look okay." Aerwyn pushed. "I can tell you're down Ula. What's up?"

"You're always with Lachlan," Ula said.

"I guess so," Aerwyn responded.

"Do you like him or something?" Ula asked.

"Um, yeah… as a friend. Why? Do you?"

"Well a little. But that's not why I'm mad." There was silence.

"Why are you mad then?" Aerwyn prodded.

"You seem to have forgotten about me… and you just hang out with him," she said quickly.

"Oh…" Aerwyn thought for a moment about her next words. "You seem to have forgotten about me, and just want to talk about princess stuff with Puakai."

Ula looked up from her crab. "That's because you are with Lachlan all of the time." She paused, looking back at the crab, who had started to poke his little head back out from his shell. "I'm trying really hard to be brave about all of this Aerwyn… but to be truthful, I'm scared finless. You're all of I've got… I need you."

Aerwyn put her arm around her friend. "I guess I hadn't realized that Ula. You always seem like you don't need me at all."

"Well, I do."

"Well," said Aerwyn, "I'll try to be there more for you… I'm really sorry… I didn't know… you have to tell me these things." The friends hugged and all was right again, for the most part. Aerwyn made a mental note to swim with Ula all of the next day, to reassure her that she had heard her.

On the fifth day, Aerwyn noticed a small shadow ahead, that became larger and larger and clearer and clearer. That must be the ridge that bounds the Norwegian Sea, she thought. She felt relief, that their days of swimming were becoming progress, but she also felt wary about crossing such a large mass. The group made camp at the base of the ridge that night. The rocks loomed above were much taller than the cliffs that housed the City of Biscay. Aerwyn had never seen anything like them. She could barely make out lookout towers built into the walls of stone. Earendil told her that they were no longer in use, and they looked long deserted. Aerwyn wondered who had once lived here, guarding the Norwegian Sea, Atlanticans or Arcticanans, or a mix of both. After the uniting of the Five, all Atlanticans had fled south to the few settlements in or around Biscay, and all Arcticanans had fled north, to their capitol city, Is. Aerwyn remembered learning at the Academy that between this ridge and the next was an oil field and much human activity. When the Five cast the spell to create the protective barrier from the humans, there was really no reason for any mers to remain and inhabit this polluted area.

Aerwyn helped unpack the conch shell attached to her favorite seahorse, who was bright pink. She loved to pet the little guy, because he always seemed grateful for her attention and nuzzled into her hand. The other five were yellow and orange, and not as interested in her. Maybe he likes my purple skin, she thought. "You're just the nicest one" she said to the little pink seahorse, as Lachlan came up to lead him to his food. "Why thank-you" said Lachlan, and Aerwyn elbowed him with a smile. He smiled back. As he swam away, Aerwyn felt someone looking at her. It was in fact two people looking at her. She turned left and saw Ula with a concerned look on her face. She corrected it to a smile when Aerwyn turned her way. She turned away to the right to grab something from the shell and saw Fenn looking at her, with a dark look on his face. She looked down and blushed privately, she hoped. He must hate it when I smile, she thought. He shoots me these dark looks because I am just not being serious enough about this whole thing.

Because it was still light out when they made camp, Ula, Puakai, and Aerwyn decided to explore a bit and get some yearned after privacy. Fenn tried to join them, but Puakai admonished him and said that she needed to be away from him for just a few minutes. This didn't help alleviate Fenn's dark look. The mers enjoyed their few moments of freedom, exploring the side of the ridge for small flowers and stones. They settled in a small basin full of vibrant colors and soft fuzzy sea grass. Aerwyn put a beautiful blue starfish in Ula's vibrant green hair, that was in just three braids today. Aerwyn put a large red sea anemone on her head. It was so large that it fell almost over her eyes.

"Guess who I am guys," she asked.

"You're my brother!" Puakai giggled as she plucked a sea urchin from its shelter and put it on her head with four others she had picked.

"Yes, Aerwyn's most secret admirer, oooo" laughed Ula.

"Ah yes, he has captured my heart as well," joked Aerwyn.

"I don't like mermen, and I don't think I ever will." Puakai said.

"That's ridiculous" retorted Ula, "and you look ridiculous." All three mers giggled and looked at each other in their recently acquired accessories.

"Well well well, what do we have here" a cold voice interrupted. Aerwyn turned around, the orange sea anemone still on her head. It was one of the scavengers from the hotel, pointing a very sharp spear in their direction. She instinctively put her arms out to push Puakai behind her.

"What are you doing here?" Asked Ula in a strong voice. But Aerwyn could tell she was afraid because she had heard this same false tone used with Queen Ulayn, usually when she was in trouble. "We are not alone; our friends are joining us here."

"Are they?" the scavenger asked. Aerwyn could see his rotted and dulled teeth through his malicious grin. "I don't think they are. In fact, I think your camp is a half a league away, and no one can hear you here." With that, he moved closer to the mers. "All I want is the one with the crown. Give me the one that can fetch a ransom, and you others can go free. If not," he sneered, "I'll just kill all three of you and steal the crown from your comrades... As a sort of consolation prize."

Ula, Puakai, and Aerwyn instinctively backed away from the scavenger, only to find themselves at the back wall of the basin oasis, sharp coral digging into their backs. The scavenger crept closer and closer, his tail flicking slowly and deliberately. When he was about six fins away, Aerwyn, panicking, shouted out "Okay, okay! Don't hurt us. I'll tell you who the princess is." She felt Ula and Puakai tense up on either side of her. "I'm the princess." She then felt their confusion.

A look of surprise passed over the scavenger's face, but he quickly regained his bristle. "How can you be the princess? You're so…. Different."

"Well yes," Aerwyn retorted, "I am, all of the royalty in Biscay are purple. That's how you know we are royal. You should know that!" She was hedging her bets here that the scavenger had never seen Ulayn or Ula, or else he would have recognized Ula right away.

The scavenger bristled at Aerwyn's slight and barked "get over here then!"

"You don't have to do this" Ula whispered.

"Just get help" Aerwyn whispered back vehemently.

Aerwyn dislodged Puakai's fingers from the scales of her shirt and moved toward the scavenger. Her mind was racing, trying to settle on what to do next. When she was two feet from him, she could smell the rotted stench of his worn clothing and matted hair. His teeth and skin were starting to decay, the sight of which made Aerwyn sick to her stomach. She was just about out of time to think of a plan when the scavenger let out a surprised noise and toppled over. A rock bounced to the ground. No longer supported by his fins, the scavenger sank slowly to the floor of the basin. The three mers looked around to see who had thrown the rock. There was

Fenn, poised with another rock. "Maids, you get out of here! There may be more where he came from!" He shouted. "I'll stay here and tie him down."

The three mers swam as fast as they could back to camp. Both Ula and Puakai thanked Aerwyn profusely while breathing heavily through their gills. "That was very brave" said Puakai. Ula squeezed her hand. They had just gotten into the camp and were in the middle of telling the others what had happened when Fenn returned, outraged.

"What in the hydra were the three of you doing?!" he exclaimed. His outrage was painted on his face like a mask, and his orange hair stood tall. "This isn't a leisure vacation where you can play dress up." At this point, Aerwyn felt pretty foolish in her sea anemone hat, and she was pretty sure the other two felt the same way about their headpieces. Sheepishly she bowed her head, sliding the orange thing off. "Good thing I followed you." He shouted and turned on his fins.

He was followed by an angry Puakai, who Aerwyn could hear following him. "Followed us? I told you we wanted to be alone! Plus, Aerwyn saved us. She had a plan!" Aerwyn watched them recede to the outskirts of the camp, where Earendil was seated, but she couldn't hear them as they lowered their voices. Aerwyn tried to ease the minds of everyone else, who had gathered around her.

"I'm glad you're okay mate," said Folander, and put an arm around her.

"That was quick thinking," said Akemi, in a tone that made Aerwyn feel like the cold Pacificanan was finally warming to her.

Lachlan clapped Aerwyn on the back. Ula, on the other hand, received a long embrace from the jolly mer. Classic Ula, thought Aerwyn, trying not to roll her eyes.

Dinner was a quiet affair. Ula and Lachlan kept glancing at one another and glancing away. Puakai wouldn't speak to Fenn. Fenn wouldn't speak to anyone but Puakai. They all agreed that there needed to be a double guard tonight in case any additional scavengers had been following them. Aerwyn had first guard with Figgs. She quietly listened to him talk about his time at comber school, while she reviewed the events of the day in her head.

Chapter 11: Oil

The group crossed the ridge by swimming through a narrow crevice about halfway up the massive wall of stone. Swimming so far away from the protections of the sea floor and all of its vegetation gave Aerwyn a queasy feeling in her stomach, like she was suspended in emptiness. They swam at a brisk pace. Earendil warned them that the next leg of their trip might be unpleasant, due to increased human activity in the region.

They emerged from the dark coolness of the crevice to dark and murky water. Trapped in by the ridge's walls, the polluted water had nowhere to go. It felt slick on Aerwyn's skin. She found it difficult to breath in the heavy water and had the urge to wipe her gills off every few minutes to clear them out. As they clustered together at the foot of the ridge, taking stock of their supplies, Earendil instructed everyone to wrap a coral silk scarf around their necks in order to keep oil out of their gills. Aerwyn rummaged through her satchel and pulled out a beautiful emerald green scarf, patterned with sea urchins of all sizes in gold thread. It was the only scarf she brought and was saving this for a more formal occasion, but she decided it would have to do. She braided her hundreds of braids into one long braid down her back, and tied the scarf around her neck and hair. As she was doing this, she saw Figgs eyeing her hair.

When he saw that she was looking at him, he smiled apologetically and said "I'm sorry Aerwyn, I've just always thought your hair was so cool." Aerwyn smiled gratefully back.

Swimming through the Norwegian Sea was starkly different than swimming in the rest of the Atlantic Ocean. There were abandoned mer settlements at every few leagues, but no mers to be seen. Once a populated corridor, this sea was a wasteland. The sea floor was murky and gray, the coral here had lost its color and were barely holding on to their dull gray lives. Every so often, a large form would float over their heads and block the sunlight--a whale or seal perhaps, but they were too far away to see what it was. Everyone was quiet and reserved in this desolate place. It didn't seem like a setting to tell stories or even talk amongst themselves very much. The oxygen level here was so slow, that every breath was labored. No wonder all of the sea life had died out. There was no oxygen to give it life. Aerwyn had no difficulty in understanding why the former inhabitants had fled from their homes.

By noon on the second day in the Norwegian Sea, they saw the first one. It was about twenty tails tall and bright yellow. To Aerwyn it looked like a giant crab, all bent out of place. Oil was leaking out in ribbons around its top, and it made a whirring, grinding sound. Earendil called it a wellhead. After that, they saw at least one wellhead an hour. All had the same leaking ribbons floating around the top and dispersing into the sea. One of the wellheads they came upon had a long pipe attached to it. The pipe started at the wellhead and went all of the way up to the sea ceiling until Aerwyn couldn't see it anymore. The noise here was unbearable, as the wellhead and pipe made a crunching and grinding sound at their connection. The group stayed far away from it and covered their ears.

The constant noise of the wellheads was exhausting and maddening. The mers could barely converse with each other. It wasn't too long before Aerwyn felt they might have a problem. It also seemed to be becoming clear to the other mers as well. The sea horses were dragging their tails and weren't making as much time as they had the previous days. The thick oily water was too much for them to navigate, and the deafening noise confused and disoriented them. Lachlan tried to comfort them the best he could, but they were unsettled and fatigued. On the third day, Puakai started dragging her fins. Being the littlest, the pollution had affected her the most of the group. On the fourth day, the little pink sea horse moved so slowly that Lachlan untied him from the shell so that he could move without encumbrance. On the fifth day, two of the yellow sea horses didn't wake up.

Lachlan attached the second conch shell to the first, in a train. The mers traded turns dragging the shells behind their backs, as the remaining two sea horses were too weak to do so. It was miserable work. On that fifth day, Puakai was so weak, that she had to be loaded into the conch shell. She rested on top of the packages of food and apologized profusely as she gurgled the oily water in through her gills. Even with a mer pushing the shells from behind, they were now too heavy. They moved a few provisions from one shell to the other, and left one of Ulayn's conch shells behind. On the sixth day, Aerwyn vomited all of her breakfast up, and couldn't keep any other food down. They were running out of time to make it out of this sea without getting too sick to swim themselves.

On evening of the sixth day, they could see the ridge, that separated them from the Greenland Sea, rising up in the distance. This invigorated them to swim faster. By speeding up in their fatigued state, they were really just barely maintaining their speed.

Fenn traveled right next to Puakai, who was now lying huddled in the shell. He kept putting his hand on her yellow hair, and whispering to her that she was strong, and it would be okay. When he caught Aerwyn watching, she saw that he had a line of worry next to his eye brow that made him look even more haughty, but Aerwyn's heart went out to him. She tried to smile encouragingly at him, and he did kind of smile back once with appreciation.

On the seventh day, they made it to the ridge by the time it was nearly dark. Puakai was breathing so heavily that all of the mers could hear her while they swam, many fins away. She was slipping in and out of consciousness. Aerwyn herself felt terrible. She had difficulty breathing, and her whole body felt exhausted and sick. She couldn't keep any food down. She also felt like she was going a bit crazy. The noise from the wellhead prevented her from forming a thought for any longer than a few seconds. She shook her head to right herself, but the discombobulation kept creeping back in.

The rest of the group was in the same shape. As they rested amongst some greasy boulders, Earendil advised the group that they would be travelling through the night to cross the northernmost ridge, which confined the Norwegian Sea. They couldn't take much more exposure to the polluted water, and Earendil wanted them to get out as soon as possible. He directed Aerwyn to collect everyone from their resting places.

She swam around to everyone, explaining the plan and trying to provide encouragement in the form of some pretty lame jokes. She received some small smiles as her comrades collected themselves. She came upon Fenn and Puakai last. She had seen Fenn swim behind a large boulder, away from the group. When she came upon them, she felt as if she had intruded on someone naked. Fenn was holding his little sister in his arms. His back muscles were tight, and his slim but muscular arms looked stronger than Aerwyn had remembered. His guard was completely down, and lines of worry covered his normally stoic face. He was whispering to his little sister, and she rested with her eyes closed. To give him some warning that she was there, Aerwyn coughed a few bubbles through her gills quietly. Fenn looked up. Disturbed from what he thought was a completely private moment, his face did not yet have its typical protective sternness. In its place Aerwyn saw a face full of love and concern. "Um, sorry to intrude… but Earendil says we have got to get over tonight… Then we can rest," She said. "I don't know why he thinks we need rest," she continued, shrugging her shoulders and feebly holding up her oil coated arms, "But I guess I'd take it." Fenn smiled politely at her lame joke and nodded. He then turned back to his sister, gathering her in his arms and lifting her, to swim her back to the group.

Travelling over the ridge in the dark was difficult. The angler fish only provided so much light in the murky water, and Aerwyn kept hitting her fins on the sides of the rock, bruising herself. The crossing took several hours, and by the time they had descended, the first rays of light were streaming into the ocean. The water on this side of the ridge was decidedly cleaner, and the relief of the mers was palatable. Before they rested at all, Earendil made them scrub themselves with sea sponges until every speck of oil was off. They had landed in an abandoned village, so they all went their separate ways to find privacy to rid themselves of the humans' pollution.

Behind a rundown stone house, Aerwyn had to discard her soiled scarf and green fish scale shirt and put on the only remaining clothing she had left, a long-sleeve green and silver fish scale shirt. She scrubbed the little coral necklace clean, and replaced it around her neck. She scrubbed her arms, face, torso, and tail. She rubbed the sponge lightly on the delicate skin of her gills. Her hair took much more work. She ran the sponge through her hair at least a hundred times, until there was no more oil on her little braids. During this precious alone time, she could not help her mind from wandering to Fenn's arms, and how strong they looked. Her mind wandered to what those arms were doing now with the cleaning process. She tried to shake the image of his face, absent its stern shield and full of love for his sister, but it kept coming back. The thought that she had misjudged him nagged at her.

The group had hunkered down, along with the seahorses, in a large abandoned home. Day and night melded together as they hunkered down and slept for three days--only awaking to trade watch shifts and eat the small amounts of bland food that their ruined stomachs could handle.

Chapter 12: The Academy

As Aerwyn lay in her hammock in that abandoned house, exhausted, her mind wandered sluggishly. She thought about her days as a competitive swimmer at the Academy. The Biscay Academy was the only school in Atlantica and had been since the last remaining one outside of the city limits had shut down fifty years ago when the country mers had moved closer for safety and resources. All mers had to attend the Academy, starting at age 7 up until age 17. It was a beautiful building in a network of caves. Each room was adorned with centuries old stone carvings. Students and professors alike would float around the classroom, reciting memorized histories and learning skills to prepare them for a life in the ocean.

Aerwyn had just graduated the term prior. She studied mer history and ocean science her first five years. The second five years were supposed to be more directed studies, focusing on subjects that would prepare her for a specific career path. Ula had studied mer management, and Figgs and Folander had studied combing several years prior. They had been the first in their class that year. The combers were always the coolest kids in the school because they were good at everything. There were other tracks too, such as farming, hunting, education, craftsmanship, food preparation, and wellness. The Academy also had a track called mer relations, but no one took that anymore, and the poor old professor would have to guest lecture about the importance of relationships with the other oceans to various history classes.

Aerwyn was secretly interested in becoming a comber, but she was intimidated by her fellow students who took that tract. Instead, Aerwyn pieced together a tract that she called human studies. There had been many mers who followed the path of human studies before the 1800s, but the profession had died off. Now there were no teaching positions or ambassadorships for the area. Still, that was what she was interested in, and her eccentric grandmother didn't say no. That led to Aerwyn not having much to do after her 17th birthday and graduation from the Academy. Ula reminded her that she would always have a job at the palace, that she could be her advisor on all matters, love and state, but Aerwyn wanted to find something to do in her own right. She hadn't found anything though. She had asked the Head of the Academy if they needed a professor to teach human studies, but he said Biscay policy prohibited him from expanding the limited program. Instead, she spent her time after graduation reading with Ula in the royal library. Coventina didn't seem to mind, so Aerwyn felt no pressure to find a job.

Aerwyn loved learning about the human world. Humans fascinated her. She loved to escape into tales of human life. There were romances that took place during massive wars, mountain climbers who had to cling to the mountains to make it to the top, boats that floated on top of the ocean, airplanes that flew with humans inside, and men that ruled instead of women. These stories took her away from her own struggles--that she was purple, that she didn't know what she wanted to do with her life after the Academy, or that Biscay had been on a fish-watch for two years in a row and their food supply was not getting any better. The humans always seemed to have food, and there always seemed to be romance--even for the different ones. In fact, the humans celebrated the different ones. There, in the human world, she would be celebrated, not tolerated. This fact alone made Aerwyn secretly think that the humans must not be as bad as they were made out to be. There must have been some misunderstanding that led the Five to cast the spell preventing contact. She didn't voice these opinions though, given how controversial the subject was.

What Aerwyn missed almost as much as learning about the human world was swimming competitively for the Academy. She wasn't the fastest swimmer, but she often won the distance events. If she set her mind to it, most times she felt like she could swim forever. When she felt like she couldn't, she remembered what Coventina said: "If your mind is across the finish line, your fins will follow." She used this strategy when she felt fatigued. Coventina was full of these helpful phrases.

She had originally joined the swim team at age 13, after dominating the junior relay race at the festival with Ula every year. On the team, she immediately was one of the better swimmers. There she met a mer named Argo. Argo had dark green hair and the most beautiful dark green skin she had ever seen. He was good. He also was one of the few mers that took the time to talk to Aerwyn at school. He was funny and nice, and she developed a huge crush on him. One day, after swim practice, Aerwyn had the brilliant idea to tell him that she liked him. An act of spontaneity that she instantly regretted. He was nice about it, but it turned out he liked Ula. Ula refused to give him the time of day after he snubbed Aerwyn. Thank goodness she had Ula, or she would have had a very lonely Academy experience. When Aerwyn had told Coventina about this, Coventina had rolled her eyes--she didn't think Aerwyn needed Ula. But she didn't live with purple skin Aerwyn thought.

At one time, Aerwyn had hoped that she could race competitively as a career, but that was before she learned that the Aequorial Games were really the only chance to earn a living as a professional athlete, and they were never coming back. There really was no life for a swimmer outside of Biscay, or inside of Biscay. That was just another reason why Aerwyn ended up not having any career plans in the months following her matriculation from the Academy last year. At least, after this quest, she could add combing to the possible careers list again.

She sighed as she rolled over in her hammock. I get it now she thought. Mers complain about Biscay being a shadow of its former glory, but this abandoned town, all of those abandoned towers on the ridges… where are those mers now? Had they come to Biscay so long ago that the desolation out here was no longer discussed? What about the sea creatures who lived near those oil fields? The lone turtle or fish that she saw, nuzzling the blackened sea grass for nutrients, its body slick and greasy. Did they feel sick like this? Or were they used to it now? The humans must know that they are hurting us down here. They must know they are hurting the wild sea life at least, even if they have forgotten about us.

Aerwyn turned her head to look at the other sleeping mers. Earendil was the only one awake. His silvery loose hair floating in the water as he serenely kept post. She had a new respect for the Pacificanans, finally making a decision to do something about their diminishing habitat. That took a lot of guts. She felt real sadness for the first time for the mers, the scientists and historians and activists, who had embarked from Pacificana initially. How many had they lost? Seven? After hearing their tale of crossing the Panama Canal, Aerwyn was grateful they wouldn't have to do that--only the seasoned combers had made it through. She was glad that Atlantica had joined. She wondered if perhaps Ulayn had been expecting this, or preparing for it on her own in some way. Aerwyn yawned. She wondered again why in the stormy sea Coventina had volunteered her for this. At least she was pulling her own weight now at least, after the jellyfish incident. I really hope the other three kingdoms are as willing to join up as we were, she thought, as she drifted back to sleep.

The mers stayed in the abandoned home for a whole week. While Aerwyn and the rest felt able to travel after three days of rest, Puakai and Earendil were too weak to move for a while, and Fenn insisted they wait until they were back in top form. Earendil was still ashen looking when they loaded up the remaining shell and horse, and had lost a significant amount of weight, but he remained silent and stoic. Now, the seriousness of the task at hand fell heavily on the minds and hearts of all the mers.

Chapter 13: The Greenland Sea

The travel now was slow going, with Earendil and Puakai weakened and the rest still recuperating from the illness caused by the oil fields. They were now in the Greenland Sea.

"This area of the Greenland Sea is well known for whales and sharks" Folander was explaining to Aerwyn as they swam along. "Earendil is having us swim a little deeper to avoid any confrontation." He looked sidelong at Aerwyn, and then said more quietly "I'm not so sure The Deep is any safer."

"Have you been there before" whispered Aerwyn.

"Only once. I swam to the bottom of the continental slope once hunting for Poseidon's Feast on one of my first missions as a comber with Ulayn's staff. I couldn't see very well, as there is no light in there, but it was interesting. I felt the cold come up from the depths, and, you know, as mers we barely register the most extreme temperature changes. I also couldn't smell anything. It was like the whole Deep was devoid of smells. Which I thought was weird."

Aerwyn could still smell by the time they had reached the edge of the continental shelf. By the time they made it down the continental slope, which took a whole day of swimming next to the steep sand and rock, she couldn't smell. The descent had been one of the creepier things she had ever done. It felt like, as they crept lower and lower, the darkness swallowed them up. She could feel that the water was colder--something that she had not experienced before. Her whole body pricked up, and her muscles felt just a little bit tighter. It was also very dark. Although she could see alright in dark places, due to her eyes being accustomed to living so far from sunlight, she could not see in places devoid of all light. In The Deep, the mers could only see by the light of the angler fish.

When they made it to the Abyssal Plains, most of the mers barely spoke, but when they did, it was in whispers or hushed tones, as if they didn't belong this far into the sea. Aerwyn swam with Lachlan in back with the seahorses. They both tried to distract from the gloom by talking. She was in the middle of telling him about the first time she had heard humans existed, and how she thought that their legs were just another set of arms where their fins should be, when Ula, curious as to what her best friend and the muscular comber were doing, joined them. Immediately, Lachlan's demeanor changed. He became much more serious, and much less inclined to laugh at Aerwyn's jokes.

Soon it became apparent that they kept stealing glances at each other. Aerwyn bowed out, referencing a need to talk to Akemi about something, to give her friend privacy. As she continued along, alone, she felt a twinge of disgust for Lachlan. How could he so easily change who he was around Ula? It was a mistake too, she laughed to herself, Ula could see through that stuff.

The other mers had started a similar strategy of talking to defeat the overwhelming silence. Ahead of her, Fenn and Earendil were in some heated debate, probably about the ethics of magic--she rolled her eyes. Figgs and Folander were talking about their family, and Folander was certainly missing his family. Akemi and Puakai were talking about what they thought Arcticana would be like. And who knows what Lachlan and Ula were discussing in those low intense whispers. Aerwyn felt very lonely in that moment, and missed Coventina. Coventina would have the right thing to say right now--like "it doesn't matter if you fit in, it only matters what you sit in" or something silly that would cheer Aerwyn up. Thinking about her grandmother brought tears to her eyes. I wonder if she is so very lonely? She thought. Immersed in her own thoughts, Aerwyn fell so far back, that she could barely make out the group in the darkness. She really didn't care. No one noticed that she wasn't there.

Coventina had been so eager to volunteer Aerwyn for this. It made sense. Coventina was always looking for ways to expand

130

Aerwyn's life. She had wanted her to swim competitively so that she could "feel the sea in her hair and get more out of life." Aerwyn thought she kind of understood that one. When she was racing, she pulled from everywhere--her body, her mind, her heart. Is that what she wanted her to do now? Aerwyn gathered herself, "I won't be sorry for myself," she said aloud, "at least I know Coventina would want that much from me." At that, Aerwyn picked up speed. She couldn't see the mers at all, but she knew she was on their track because she could feel the bubbles from their swimming bumping into her face.

All of a sudden, from the darkness she heard a loud commotion ahead. Figgs' voice rang out, "It's coming!" She stopped on her fins. She couldn't really see what was happening, but she sensed movement to the left, and swam behind a large stump of slime covered stone. She sensed it rather than saw it. A white, massive, slippery body, about twelve feet long, slowly glided past her, like a large flotsam making its way down the current. Squid! thought Aerwyn with panic.

Her stomach leapt into her mouth, but instinct told her not to rush into the melee happening in front of her. Instead, she quickly flitted from rock to rock, remaining unseen. She got close enough to make out what was happening. The entire band was surrounded by a giant squid. It was slowly circling the group, all of whom had their spears drawn, tentacles swirling and churning the water. Lachlan stabbed out at one tentacle that happened to get too close. The spear bounced off the slick thick skin, without penetration. After that, the fear on the faces of her comrades was palpable.

Aerwyn's mind was racing in panic when she heard screams. Black ink was filling the water around the group. She pulled her spare shirt from the satchel slung around her shoulders and tied it around her face just as the ink was washing over her. She heard Puakai scream. Fenn called out with panic: "Puakai! Puakai!" Aerwyn knew the squid was passing back by her, because she could sense the immense form and heard Puakai's muffled struggles. Unable to see, but not confident the ink was gone yet, Aerwyn turned to follow the squid without sight.

She followed the sound of its movements, trying not to bump into anything. The squid had a wide berth, so she didn't hit much. It felt like they were going deeper. She removed her shirt from around her head after a few minutes and squinted her eyes. The ink had cleared. She could barely see the squid's white body a few tails ahead. She could see bright yellow hair sticking out of a tentacle, and fear gripped her.

After a few minutes of Aerwyn following it, the squid slowed its pace. Then, without pausing, it slunk into a crevice in the cliffs. Aerwyn took off her blindfold. Its lair. The squid flung its treasure in the corner of the cave and retreated further in until Aerwyn could not see it anymore. This sparked Aerwyn's curiosity. I wonder why he is not eating her right now? She thought. Puakai's form on the ground was motionless. Aerwyn hovered at the mouth of the cave for a moment and then backed out to think. She had to get Puakai out of the cave without disrupting the resting squid. She couldn't risk the squid knowing she was there in case he squirted his ink again. If he blinded her, there would be no way she could make it away from the squid. At the same time, there was not a lot of time to orchestrate any kind of creative plan, so whatever she needed to do, she needed to do it fast.

Aerwyn floated to the bottom of the cave floor to her belly and inch by inch crept into the cave, flicking her tail imperceptibly. She made it to Puakai's body and wrapped her arms around it. She then turned to the cave opening and started inching out, dragging the limp body with her and keeping low and out of the periphery of the squid, wherever he was. She was just about to the mouth of the cave when she heard water churning in the rear of the lair. Instantly, she gave up trying to be stealthy and pulled Puakai as hard as she could through the mouth of the cave.

She looked back and could just make out the giant white squid bolting after her--she had been spotted. Fear struck Aerwyn like a wave over her brain and heart, but she pushed it down into her belly, where it took hold. She swam as fast as she could for a few tail lengths, but she knew that outpacing the massive squid once outside the confines of his cave was untenable. She spotted a dark shape in the cliff to her left and zoomed toward it. She felt it with her hand, it was an opening. She shoved Puakai into the crevice and followed. She pushed her further and further back. Just as they hit the back of the crevice, the squid's white slippery tentacle slipped into the crack. Further and further in it slipped, until it was three inches from Aerwyn's shaking body. And then it stopped. It felt around for several seconds, prodding the walls of the crevice, just barely missing the mers. The seconds felt like hours, and Aerwyn didn't move a muscle. Then, frustrated, he withdrew his probe. Aerwyn released her breath in slow bubbles out of her gills and slumped back with relief.

She turned her attention to Puakai, who was still unconscious, although she was breathing slowly. Aerwyn tried to revive her, and she fluttered her eyes open. However, there was no way that she was going to be able to swim. Aerwyn didn't want to leave her in the crack by herself either, in case the squid came back. She was just going to have to wait here to see if the others would come.

The two mers sat in that cave for several hours, sitting very still. Puakai fell in and out of consciousness, and Aerwyn tried to wake her up each time, but she was dazed and exhausted and could barely move after her near suffocation from the tentacles. Aerwyn felt helpless.

Eventually, she heard a voice. It was Lachlan. She could hear him calling out Puakai's name. She sat up and yelled "Lachlan! Lachlan! We are in here!"

"Aerwyn? Is that you? Where are you?"

" We are here, in the crack in the cliff. Can you see it?"

Lachlan swam in. "Oh holy Poseidon. We have been searching for you two for hours. I was sure you were lost forever Aerwyn, since we didn't see you during the attack." He hugged her with his muscular arms, holding her close. She let her head rest on his shoulder for a moment, exhausted and relieved. He was still covered in ink, with only the areas around his eyes, mouth, nose, and gills wiped clean.

Lachlan carried Puakai back to the group's meeting spot, a little alcove in the cliff wall surrounded on all sides but one by rock and coral, while Aerwyn kept watch from behind. Earendil was the only mer there. He immediately, tucked Puakai into the conch shell and started caring for her shock with an experienced hand. Lachlan helped Aerwyn into a hammock, but she was too wound up to rest. One by one, the rest of the mers straggled in from their search attempts. When Ula came back, she rushed over to Aerwyn and gathered her in a tight hug. "Oh seven seas, I am so happy you are back!" Aerwyn felt warm inside for a moment. Then, Ula continued louder, so that everyone could hear, "Don't ever go off on your own again you crazy mer! This isn't one of your human novels." Aerwyn smiled and nodded, but she was insulted. Even her own friend thought she couldn't fend for herself?

Fenn was the last mer to get back to the meeting spot, an hour after everyone else had returned. Aerwyn felt sorry for him. He was clearly distraught and exhausted. When he spotted Aerwyn, he pricked up a little bit. "Is she here Aerwyn?" He asked immediately, his voice desperate and strained. Aerwyn nodded, and Fenn collapsed on the ground with exhaustion.

Chapter 14: The Ice Ocean

Everyone was anxious to get to Arcticana. They climbed their way up and up from abyssal plain back up to the populated continental shelf. Apparently, sharks were better than giant squid, which no weapon seemed to penetrate. Between the experience in the Norwegian oil fields and in the abyssal plain of the Greenland Sea, Aerwyn had a healthy understanding for why the mers had all settled on the continental shelf--green and rich with wildlife and beautiful scenery and far from the cold dark of The Deep.

Aerwyn kept her distance from Ula over the next few days, still annoyed that her friend had insinuated she couldn't take care of herself. Had she been jealous over the attention Aerwyn had received for outsmarting the squid? She had time to think this over because it was easy to keep her distance since Ula spent every waking moment with Lachlan and didn't seem to notice Aerwyn's hurt at all.

The mers could tell when they were getting close to the capitol city of Is when they started to see mer settlements, and their course felt like more of a path than a directionless swim. Aerwyn was so relieved to see other mers. At Earendil's instruction, she did not wave, but she did smile at the Arcticanans. The Arcticanans on the other hand did not seem that happy about seeing them. The mers on the outskirts of the capitol quickly retreated into their dwellings when the travelers appeared in their sights. Merchildren peeped out from the windows, watching the newcomers. Their homes were very charming to Aerwyn, little domed igloos made of rocks and ice. They were small and sparkly, and Aerwyn thought Coventina would love them.

In addition to the different dwellings, the mers here looked different. Just as the Pacificanans had human-colored skin with yellow and orange hair and blue fins, and the Atlanticans had green skin, fins, and hair, the Arcticanans had their own unique coloring. They all had silver fins, with varying shades of white and silver skin and hair. Their fins were more shimmery than the other mers. The women here also wore their hair long like Aerwyn's tribe, but they did not braid it. It flowed in swirls around their heads, shoulders, and backs. Aerwyn was mystified at how it wasn't in one big tangle from the salt water. She was reminded of the human novels she had read, in which most heroines had flowing long hair. All of the mers were wearing fur of some sort. As if reminded that the water had become much colder, Aerwyn shivered. Even the cold-blooded weren't impervious to extreme temperature changes.

As they got closer to the city center, they passed mers going about their daily business, all who turned to stare at the travelers. Aerwyn felt as if her purple skin must be glowing given the especially long looks she was getting. Some mers were hauling fish, some were sewing fur clothing on their doorsteps. It reminded Aerwyn of a busier, wealthier, more populated Atlantica. As the dwellings got closer together and more frequent, the outline of the castle came into view. It stopped Aerwyn and the other mers short. It was the most magnificent thing Aerwyn had ever seen. The castle was the bottom, sea immersed part of a giant iceberg. It shimmered bright blue and had windows and turrets carved into its exterior.

They were so shallow at this point that Aerwyn could see the surface. Ice was in the place where the water should have met the sky. The ice was covered with green algae, growing into the water. The algae gave the whole area a green tint. Holes where the ice had melted or been broken provided sunlight, which streamed into the water like bright tunnels. They were much closer to the surface than Aerwyn had ever been before, but she could see why the mers felt safe settling here, the ice coverage made everything very private.

The entrance to the castle was about a league above the city, as the glacier did not reach all of the way to the sea floor. Guarding the entrance were two mermen, sitting on the backs of two beautiful, and terrifying, orca whales. Aerwyn had never seen an orca whale before. They were wonderful. They also were a little ferocious looking. There had been a time when Atlantica had domesticated some of the smaller whales for purposes of travel and even companionship. But the whale population started to diminish, and the Atlanticans had freed their whales to assist the dwindling species in re-populating their ocean. The presence of whales here gave Aerwyn the feeling of stepping back in time, to when mers and humans belonged together in the world.

As they got closer to the castle, Aerwyn could see that the exterior of the glacier was carved with intricate depictions of sea life--from magnificent mers in full armor, to sea urchins and starfish, the entire surface was patterned with a story. The homes closer to the castle became more and more fancy, some were carved into surrounding ice chunks, growing from the top of the sea, others were built with what looked like stones, but were actually large blocks of ice, pieced together. Everything was decorated. There was not a surface that wasn't carved, ornamented, or gilded. Aerwyn's heart filled with the beauty of her surroundings. What a place!

Once they reached the door to the castle, the finsmen approached them. Aerwyn had a difficult time hiding her shock. The guards had two tails, that split from half way down their fins. "Welcome to Arcticana" said the one on the left, "We've been expecting you."

Chapter 15: The Assembly

As they swam through the entrance to the castle, Aerwyn grabbed for Ula's hand, forgetting her anger. If the outside was ornate and sparkling, the inside was downright baroque and glittering. Everywhere she looked was an ice, silver, diamond, or platinum sculpture. They looked at each other with excitement as if to say What had we been so apprehensive about? This place was great! The finsmen took the group to what they called the assembly hall, which was a giant room with arched ceilings and glittering chandeliers made from angler fish and blue algae floating around in glass orbs. The queen was seated facing the hall with five advisors on each side of her. As they approached and bowed, she gestured for them to be seated on the crystal seats in front of her.

It wasn't until Aerwyn focused in on the queen that she remembered and acutely felt her own shabbiness. The queen, who was about Aerwyn's age, had a glittering silver tail, pale silver skin, and pure white, flowing hair, loosely curling around her shoulders, unaffected by the salt water that snarled Aerwyn's own black locks. She wore a sheer cape, trimmed with white fur and a necklace of many strands of hundreds of diamonds that was so large that it covered her breasts. But other than the necklace, Aerwyn wasn't sure she was wearing anything else under that sheer cape. A glance at Figgs beside her, who was staring at that very spot with his mouth open, confirmed her hypothesis. The queen's crown was a fairly simple affair comparatively. She wore a silver circlet, much like Aerwyn's, around her head. Unlike Aerwyn's, it was studded with diamonds. The only part about her that wasn't silver or white were her eyes, which were emerald green. She took Aerwyn's breath away. Aerwyn looked down at her own clothing. She was wearing the only shirt she had left, the green fish scale one, and it was worse for wear. Her hair could stand to be re-braided, and she was sure she was covered in oil and ink. The queen didn't seem to notice.

It was one of the advisors who spoke first. "Welcome to Arcticana, travelers! We are overjoyed to share our home with you while you are on your journey. Unless, of course, this is your destination, then you would be welcomed to stay. You will have not heard, but six months ago we lost our beloved Queen Issy. Her daughter, as you see here, Queen Gwylfai, has ascended the throne. But she still needs much guidance as she is young and became mute at the untimely passing of her mother." He paused. None of the travelers really knew what to do, so Aerwyn just followed Earendil's lead and bowed her head, murmuring "may the sea engulf your soul." The advisor

143

continued: "Please tell, what is the news of the other oceans? I see that you have Atlanticans and Pacificanas among you. And… another as well." Aerwyn flitted her tail uncomfortably. She was annoyed--she was Atlantican too, regardless of her purpleness. Ula rested her hand reassuringly on Aerwyn's arm.

Earendil bowed to the queen deeply and then told an abridged version of the events that got them there today. He told her about how they sought to break the spell of the Five Eldoris in order to commune with the humans to protect their ocean home. Aerwyn was more interested this time, since she now actually cared about the result. Earendil explained his theory about how a female mer in the royal line was the most likely to have the power to break the spell. When he spoke about the Eldoris objects, the advisors' interest piqued. "So, you have travelled with the Eldoris all this time?" One asked eagerly and with enough of a touch of greed on his voice that Aerwyn felt her coral necklace burning on her chest. She was sure Ula felt the same about her decoy crown.

When they finished their tale, the advisors asked for a moment, and they were led out of the assembly hall. It seemed like hours that they waited outside the door. The combers of the group, Lachlan, Akemi, Figgs, and Folander, were particularly restless.

"I don't like this place" said Folander, "it gives me the wiggling eels."

"Ahh, it's fine." replied Lachlan, "but I don't much like those stone-faced advisors."

"What do you think is the deal with that silent queen? No king about?" asked Figgs.

They were called back in. Again, the first advisor spoke while the queen looked silently on. "We will join you in friendship in your quest. We cannot commence immediately, as we will need to arrange leadership if our dear queen leaves us temporarily. We would ask that you wait two days to depart to your next destination. During that time, we will hold a ball celebrating your quest!" He said, smiling and opening his arms wide. Earendil grumpily consented. Aerwyn had to stifle a little snort. Earendil at a ball!

They were each led to a room in a different part of the castle, as it had been explained that there were no quarters that could house all of them. Fenn insisted on staying with Puakai, to the point of rudeness, and the guard leading them to their rooms was bullied into consenting. Aerwyn was happy to have some alone time. She was still annoyed at Ula for insinuating that she couldn't fend for herself, even after she had saved

Puakai from the squid. She was even more annoyed that her friend didn't seem to notice.

Her room was magnificent. She plopped down on the bed and took a look around. In this room, the walls of the ice castle were gilded with glass tiles, so she could see the blue ice beneath them but could not touch the ice. There was a chandelier similar to the chandeliers in the assembly room. It was a giant glass orb, containing swirling blue bioluminescent algae, and it made the room sparkle with blue. The bed was in the shape of a hammock, but was also made of glass. It had dark blue puffy looking anemones piled up on it and was topped off with a giant white seal fur throw. It felt incredibly luxurious, even if she hadn't been on the swim for so long. The rest of the room contained a closet for her belongings, made of glass and gilded with silver, a small round table with two chairs of the same material, and a long mirror. The table had a white coral vase holding an immense electric blue sea anemone. Aerwyn swam over and sat at the table, fingering the long blue strands of the anemone. What a place!

As she lay back, truly alone for the first time in weeks, Aerwyn mulled over the events of the trip so far. She definitely felt close to all of the mers on the quest, even Earendil and Fenn. Their struggles had created a closeness among them that hadn't been there when they started. Aerwyn didn't feel like she was benefitting the group per se, but she didn't feel like she was a burden anymore either. That incident with the squid had seemed to increase everyone's respect for her. Even Figgs and Folander, who had always been nice to her, had been confused as to why she had been along with these combers, scholars, and royalty. At least now she was earning her keep. She rolled her eyes thinking about Ula. How annoying! Ula hadn't done anything compared to her this trip, and she felt like she could say that? She could be so condescending! As she drifted into a light sleep, thoughts of Fenn's arms tenderly holding his sister rose up as well, but she pushed them down. Since she saved Puakai, he didn't scowl at her as much. But he disliked her, that was clear. She wasn't so sure what she felt about him either.

It wasn't long before a knock came at the door. One of the two-tailed guards was waiting at it with a tray full of steaming hot food. The guard indicated to Aerwyn that Earendil had requested that they all dine in their room in order to get rest. Tired, hungry, and happy to have the solitude, Aerwyn was grateful. She stuffed her face full of the delicacies of the north that she had never tasted before and quickly fell asleep, her full belly and thoughts as comfortable companions.

148

Chapter 16: A Day Alone

Aerwyn awoke the next day when daylight started streaming into her window. She lay luxuriously under the fur throw for some time, savoring the comfort. When she finally felt restless enough to get up and do something with her day, she got up and swam to her window. The view below was astounding. Because the castle was carved into the bottom of an immense ice berg, it seemed to float above the rest of Is. The homes of the Arcticana mers were dense at the foot of the castle and extended like fallen ice cubes away from it in all directions. The sea life was prolific, and the mers were active about their days. Is appeared to be more populated than Atlantica and more prosperous as well. Maybe when all is said and done, I'll come back here and live, she thought.

Aerwyn brushed the scales on her shirt, and attempted to polish it up a bit. She put it on and headed out of her room. Her room was off of a long tunnel in the ice. There were other doors off of the tunnel, but she didn't know where they led to. She floated around for a while, looking for some sign of the others. Perhaps they were resting as well? Eventually she made her way to the first level of the castle, where the assembly room was. She entered, and saw Earendil eating with some of the advisors from the prior day. He nodded to her but didn't invite her over, so she backed out. She wandered around for a while longer, but with no sign of the others she felt uneasy about venturing beyond the castle. She made her way back to her room.

When she got there, the queen was waiting for her, as were several attendants and an advisor. "Her majesty desired to come by personally to offer you my services to prepare for the ball this evening," the advisor said after Aerwyn bowed. "We have just a few hours to prepare," he continued, "but I'm not sure that is enough time" he finished, pointedly looking at Aerwyn's disheveled braided hair. The queen smiled coldly at Aerwyn as the advisor criticized Aerwyn's appearance. She looked as if she wanted to say something to Aerwyn, but being mute, could not. "Thank you for attentions, Queen Gwylfai" Aerwyn smiled "it has been a very long time since I have felt like I look presentable, and I'm very much looking forward to feeling that way tonight." The Queen nodded and glided out with the advisor and all but one of the attendants, perhaps to the next traveler's room. Aerwyn rolled her eyes. Appearances were very important to these people.

Aerwyn truly enjoyed the preparation for the ball. It did take about three hours total, but she was able to converse with the Arcticanan attendant the entire time. The attendant, also had a silver tail and silver skin, but her hair was a dark silver, close in color to Aerwyn's own black hair. She told Aerwyn about her life growing up in Is and how wonderful life was under Queen Issy. She hinted that life might not be as wonderful now, but when Aerwyn pressed, she wouldn't say anything further. She asked Aerwyn about Atlantica, and what life was like there.

She unbraided all of Aerwyn's braids and meticulously brushed out the snarls. Then she slathered her hands in oil from a crystal flask and ran them throughout Aerwyn's hair, for what seemed like an hour, coating every single strand. She explained that it was oil from seal blubber that the mers in Arcticana used in their hair to prevent it from snarling. They just had to reapply the oil once a week, and never had to worry about braiding their hair. She then placed Aerwyn's silver circlet on the top of the flowing mass of black hair. Aerwyn loved the effect, and made a mental note to snag a flask of the oil before they departed. It certainly did accentuate the different color of her hair, but it felt soft and flowing and luxurious, like what a human standing in the wind must feel like. The attendant had sprinkled small pearls in the black locks, and they peeked out at Aerwyn when she turned her head in the mirror.

The attendant made her take off her shirt and helped her bathe, and then she assisted her in oiling her fins, so that they were a brilliant shiny purple. She scrubbed her skin clean, removing any of the oil, ink, and general algae residues that had accumulated over the past few weeks. Finally, she rubbed a salve all over Aerwyn's fins, torso, arms, and face, that was full of glitter and made Aerwyn sparkle. She tried to take off Aerwyn's necklace to polish it, but Aerwyn remembered Coventina's warning and politely refused.

Finally, she brought out from her satchel of beauty products a sheer, long-sleeved coral silk shirt. The shirt was cut so that it was off of her shoulders, with long flowing sleeves. Fluffy white seal fur lined the large neck, cuffs, and bottom, which reached halfway down Aerwyn's tail. The attendant slipped it on over Aerwyn's head, and stood back admiring. Aerwyn looked down. Her breasts were totally exposed. She looked at the attendant, who was wearing a semi sheer vest, and then back at herself.

"So..." she said, wondering how not to be offensive, "our culture covers up" she held her breasts in her hands "these."

The attendant laughed "oh don't you worry, you'll fit right in here, no need to be embarrassed." Aerwyn wasn't that sure.

When the attendant finally left, Aerwyn slipped the shirt off and tied a white silk scarf that she found in the dresser around her chest and then put the sheer shirt back on over it. Hopefully that will thread the needle between politeness and her own cultural norms, she thought. The attendant had told her to wait for an escort to bring her down, so she admired herself in the mirror for a few minutes. She liked the look. But it didn't take long once the attendant left for another knock on the door. The two-tailed finsman was there and offered her his arm. Aerwyn lost the confidence she had admiring herself in the mirror but moments ago, and felt that her purple skin, unmuted through the sheer shirt, was exposed in a way that she never let it be in Atlantica.

Chapter 17: A Ball

Her escort didn't speak as he guided Aerwyn to the top of the castle, to the great hall. They entered and Aerwyn caught her breath. This room was even more magnificent than the assembly hall. It was lit with blue and green bioluminescent algae, and sparkled with their light. There were hundreds of crystal beads hanging from the ceiling, and intricate carvings covered the glass enclosed ice walls.

As she swam in she saw Ula, who was lingering alone near a pile of desserts on a nearby table. Aerwyn thanked her escort and swam to Ula. Her escort followed her, until Ula waved her hand at him and said "please, that's enough." He flitted away, a little confused at the rejection. She saw that Ula too had found the sheer shirt to be too much, and was wearing a white star fish over each breast. Before saying anything, they just looked at each other and laughed. When that laugh died out, Ula wordlessly pointed to Akemi at the other end of the room, who was wearing a sheer cape and a high pony tail. She had her arms crossed uncomfortably over her bare breasts. They laughed harder than they had in weeks. Poor Akemi. All of a sudden, the anger that Aerwyn had been feeling toward Ula faded and they were back to normal.

Ula and Aerwyn traded stories about their evenings and ball preparation. Ula looked beautiful with her emerald green hair flowing around her. As Earendil had directed prior to arrival, she did not wear her traditional headdress that indicated her royal heritage. She was wearing a silver sheer dress with black fur cuffs and tiny diamonds in her hair. Not for the first time Aerwyn felt a trickle of jealously at Ula's physical advantages. She shook it off--Ula couldn't help it.

Everyone was seated for dinner, and one of the advisors welcomed the guests of honor. A rich, magenta colored dulse wine was poured and everyone toasted to the travelers. Ula drank deep, but Aerwyn turned to the food instead with great anticipation. There was meat from sea lions, seals, and penguins on the table. Aerwyn had only ever had land meat once before, when Biscay's combers had uncovered a store of jerky in a sunken ship, and she was thrilled at the idea of trying the food of the humans for a second time.

The group conversed politely with the Arcticanans seated at their table. Aerwyn felt warm with congeniality of it all. But, when she looked up where Queen Gwylfai was sitting, still covered in her diamonds, a weird feeling passed slowly through her. The queen munched slowly on the food, but looked like she took no pleasure from it. While her advisors seated around her conversed, she stared off into the distance. Although she was around Aerwyn's age, she seemed older and more refined. She also seemed deeply depressed.

Aerwyn ate all of the things that she had never seen before and felt very content enjoying the luxury of the Arcticanans. Even Atlantica's own Brine Festival or Poseidon's Feast couldn't compare to the amount of food and decoration at this welcoming ball. As soon as she leaned back, fuller of food than she had been in weeks, an attendant whisked her plate away. A sea horn band started playing, and the Arcticana mers wandered to the dance space in the center of the room. Since there were just shy of one hundred mers invited to the ball, the prestigious of the Is community, the dance floor filled up quickly.

Aerwyn remained at the table and relaxed with Ula. Despite feeling very self-conscious in her sheer shirt, she had no complaint except that Ula was distracted from their conversation by Lachlan, who was flirting with a group of silver-haired bare-chested mers and soaking up the attention. To distract her friend from the slight, Aerwyn tried to point out the other mers from their group who were also being bamboozled by the beautiful Arcticana. All were surrounded by flirtatious mers. Figgs was soaking in the attention with glee and was seemed to be regaling his admirers with tales of being a comber, as his arms were gesturing wildly. Folander was uncomfortably trying to escape the attention, swimming away whenever a mermaid would approach him. Fenn was rather sullenly sitting while two beautiful mers who had given up talking with him and were talking over him. Akemi was talking with just one mer, and the two merwomen seemed to be hitting it off, as their heads were bent close. It must have been the weeks on the sea that made everyone glad to be around new people who were both friendly and attractive.

"Maybe we would be getting some attention if you didn't scare off all of these mermen who try to approach us with your bristles Ula," Aerwyn said.

"I'm not the only one who doesn't want this stupid flattery. Check Fenn out over there," replied Ula. Aerwyn turned to look back at Fenn. He had creeped even further away from his female companions. "He is pretty handsome, when he is all cleaned-up," continued Ula. Aerwyn rolled her eyes, Ula better not be moving on to Fenn now that she was slighted by Lachlan. She caught herself in that thought and wondered why she cared.

"Really? I don't see it. He is so… rigid," responded Aerwyn. But as she was replying, Fenn caught her looking at him. When he met her eyes, he gave her an uncharacteristic smile. Aerwyn couldn't help herself from having a blush creep up her neck. She quickly looked away. What was that for? She thought.

"Perhaps he is a little handsome," she conceded to her friend, who was looking at her and the blush with a quizzical look. "But he is just so stiff. Not a charming one at all."

"Charming isn't everything" said Ula as she nodded at Lachlan. "This one is charming, but also puts on quite a show. What's real and what is not? I don't know."

The mers were interrupted from their discussion of Lachlan and his flirtations by Fenn, who suddenly appeared looming over them. "Aerwyn, do you want to dance?" He asked, as the band started playing a different song. Taken aback, Aerwyn resorted to her politeness and said yes without even thinking about it. Fenn took her hand formally and pulled her to the dance floor. Aerwyn looked back at Ula, who had a mischievous grin on her face.

The song was slow, and Fenn held her waist with one hand and guided her around the space slowly with the other. He was a head taller than her, and Aerwyn didn't really know where to look, so she focused her eyes over his shoulder. They danced for a few moments in an awkward silence. Now that she was in them, she couldn't help but think of Fenn's arms around his sister. They were just as firm as she had imagined, and she felt her belly flip with a pang of attraction to him. She shook her head, as if to get the thought out of it. She couldn't be attracted to him, not after he had embarrassed her so in front of her tribe. She felt an immediate need to clear the waters.

"Aerwyn I…" Fenn started to say as Aerwyn said quickly at the same time "You were wrong about me."

She continued, not letting him speak, "What you said about me… I do have valuable things to add to this quest. And you shouldn't have said I don't." Fenn, surprisingly, smiled encouragingly in response. "I… am…" for some reason she could not think of exactly what she added at this very moment, all of these uncharacteristic smiles were throwing her off.

"You're quick on your fins and you hold this rag tag group together better than Earendil can," Fenn answered for her.

Aerwyn met his eyes. "Yes… I guess so," she replied somewhat awkwardly.

"I was just going to say sorry about that actually. Sorry that I just judged you right off. I shouldn't do that as much as I do. And I got it wrong, so that doesn't help either." He gave her a small sheepish smile.

"Well. Thanks." She replied. After a few silent moments, she continued, "It's okay. I'm sure I would be very worried about some random mer being tasked with guarding Ula, if I were in your position." Over his face passed a hint of the look she had seen when he was caring for Puakai back in the oil. She tried to save him the embarrassment of such emotional exposure, and quickly followed up with "Plus, I totally judged you too. You're definitely not as… severe… and unsparing as I thought."

Fenn laughed, and his face became handsome, "Severe? Unsparing? Me? Wow, we did get off on the wrong fin!"

Aerwyn's stomach had butterflies in it. Coventina would be so proud of her for defining how she wanted be treated! But there were butterflies there for something else too--she couldn't deny that she was grateful that Fenn saw he had been mistaken for the sole reason that she really liked how strong his arms were.

He continued, "You've saved Puakai… twice now. I can't ever thank you enough for that." Aerwyn looked up into his face, and his dark eyes stared back in seriousness again. "Puakai is all that I have. Our mother has gone into the deep end and is no longer the mer she once was… If I lose Puakai too…" He paused for a moment as if lost in thought and then continued "I don't know what is going to happen once we have all of the Eldoris. And we have to do that…. Thing… I want to do the right thing and let her do it… that's why I came here, by Poseidon! But sometimes I think I would rather avoid the risk and leave our oceans to fend for themselves. Hell, I'd rather everyone in all the seas die than just float by and watch Puakai die." He paused for a moment and then finished, "The strain between doing the right thing and the thing that feels good sometimes feels like it is too much." He looked away.

Aerwyn was unsure of what to say, but she could see the older brother's pain all over his face. She paused for a moment, thinking about her words, for once, and softly replied "You're going to have to trust her to make that choice, Fenn. Just as we all will. All we can do is try to get this thing right every step of the way. And trust ourselves to do that." She said kindly.

Fenn tightened his grip on her lower back almost imperceptibly. He looked like he wanted to say something else. He didn't. Instead, he just stared at her looking torn between gratefulness and seriousness. Aerwyn looked back. All of a sudden, Aerwyn felt the hand he had holding her waist. It felt like it burned into her skin. She was aware of her hand, holding his broad, strong shoulder, which was bare under a seal fur vest. She noticed the inch of space between them, both pushing them apart and pulling them in. She met his gaze with her own confused look. She became acutely aware of her purple skin and the sheer top, leaving almost nothing to Fenn's imagination and certainly not the extent of her purpleness. She glanced down to make sure the thin scarf was doing its job. He grasped her embarrassment and flashed her another out of character grin. They both flushed and looked away.

Suddenly the music stopped and Fenn quickly dropped his hold of her. Aerwyn thought he was going to speed away. Instead, he ran a nervous hand through his tall red hair and asked "Want to check out the view?"

The view from the balcony was similar to that of her room except now that evening had settled in, the homes were aglow with blue and green algae lanterns. They floated side-by-side on the balcony, taking in the view. Their arms touched, and Fenn didn't pull away. In fact, it seemed like he had positioned himself so that this would happen. Aerwyn's mind was awhirl. She stole a look at Fenn. With his fiery red hair and strong chin, he was more handsome than Aerwyn had initially thought, if not very serious looking at this moment. There was a noise as a finsman made his way onto the balcony. Fenn pulled Aerwyn behind a giant orca whale statue and into a rounded alcove in the exterior wall of the castle. Now they were even closer, and Aerwyn felt that push-pull again. When the guard left, for a moment Fenn didn't move any further away, and their bodies were very close as he looked down at her. They both paused there for a moment, breathing out of their gills heavily. Then, as if he put on a mask, his face changed and he leaned back. He ran a hand through his hair and boyishly quipped, "So, what was it like growing up with a mermagician grandmother?"

What felt like just minutes later, but was in fact over an hour, the pair decided to stop discussing their lives in their respective oceans and join the others. Aerwyn felt a twinge of regret. It had actually been fun hanging out with Fenn in that alcove. She felt relieved that they were friends now. There was also that confusing push-pull feeling that just wasn't going away. There was no time to think of that however, because as soon as they reentered the ballroom, an eerie vibe washed over them. What had been lively dancing and conversation was now a few mers moving around the dance area slowly, and the surrounding mers talking in hushed tones. Aerwyn scanned the room for her friends. Lachlan was there, so were Earendil, Figgs, Folander, and Akemi. They were all lethargic looking. Are they drunk? thought Aerwyn. She swam up to Figgs, whose head could barely stand up. Yes, he was certainly drunk. She looked around the room again. Where was Ula? And Puakai? She met Fenn's eyes, which revealed he was wondering the same thing. Something wasn't right.

Chapter 18: Trapped

Fenn immediately sprang into action and swam to her. "Aerwyn, you round up everyone in here… find a way to sober them up. I'll look for Puakai and Ula," he yelled in a whisper. He briskly added "back exit in thirty minutes" and swam off. Aerwyn frantically swam to each of her comrades, trying to shake them into sobriety. It seemed to be working for Akemi and Folander, both of whom had resisted drinking most of their beverages.

Once the group was together, and they were being looked at skeptically by the mers around them, Aerwyn announced quietly that something was up: "we are missing Ula and Puakai. Something doesn't feel right about this. I want each of you to go back to your rooms… DISCREETLY" she added, as Figgs started bee lining it to the exit. "Grab your stuff and let's meet at the back exit in thirty minutes." She pointed at Figgs now exiting the room "Folander, you go get your brother. Grab Akemi's stuff. Akemi, come with me… we need their queen."

Aerwyn surprised herself at her decisiveness. She couldn't help but smile as she and Akemi lingered in the hall, attempting to look gregarious and hoping to draw attention away from the others. Aerwyn searched the room for Queen Gwylfai. She was alone on her throne, her advisors all around her talking. Gwylfai was staring at Aerwyn. Aerwyn felt a prickle go down her spine. Did the queen have something to do with the absence of Puakai and Ula? How was she going to get this mer away from her advisors? A thought sprung up as she noticed the advisors were all male.

Aerwyn grabbed Akemi's hand and swam up to the queen. She bowed her head. The advisors immediately ceased their conversations and turned toward Aerwyn, staring at her. "My lady," Aerwyn started, "I have a very pressing… er… mermaid matter that needs your attention." The advisors all took a flick of the tail back awkwardly. Aerwyn almost laughed out loud. That was easier than she thought. "Would you and a translator mermaid be able to assist me?" The queen, without changing expression, beckoned to the attendant mer that Aerwyn recognized as the one who had prepared her for the ball. Aerwyn noticed the advisors all glaring at the queen and the queen putting out her hand as if to tell them to relax, it would be okay.

Aerwyn followed the queen out of the room and down the hall headed to the back entrance. Akemi was behind her. She hadn't thought out this part. Was she going to have to knock the queen out? And then drag her to the back entrance? She looked back at Akemi who had a look on her face like she wouldn't mind doing just that. Suddenly, they were pulled into a small alcove just within sight of the guarded back entrance. To her great surprise, the queen spoke.

"You must leave," she whispered frantically. "My advisors are not persuaded by your cause. In fact, they find you a threat to our peace and prosperity here. They are preparing to capture the princesses and murder the rest of you. It is best you go now, before it is too late." Her emerald green eyes were narrow and sharp.

Aerwyn was speechless. Despite the severity of this information relayed to her, all she could find herself saying was "you talk?"

Gwylfai looked impatiently at her. Akemi spoke next: "I think that has become pretty obvious that our welcome is worn out my lady. But we need you to come with us in order for this to work. I'm sorry but…" and as Akemi drew a small dagger out of her pony tail, Gwylfai put up her hands:

"Yes, yes I understand. I will come with you voluntarily…and… and do whatever needs to be done to unite the Eldoris. I believe in your cause. But you need to get me two things for me to agree to that. My twin brother… and the Eldoris…. Luckily, they are in the same spot." Gwylfai said. Information was coming at Aerwyn really quickly now. Twin brother? Where had he been this whole time? Why couldn't Gwylfai get him herself? Her questions were answered as quickly as they were generated. "He is in the dungeons. I have been forbidden from going up there, and doing so will arouse suspicion. One of you must go." Gwylfai pulled a small key from nowhere and handed it to Akemi. "Tell him I sent you, and that he needs to bring the Eldoris. He may need help. I will go appease my advisors, request to go to bed, and then wait here." She leaned back on the wall of the alcove. Akemi turned to Aerwyn.

"This sounds like something you would be good at. No one suspects you ever, Aer. Which is dumb, and we can talk about that later, but I think you should go. I'll wait here for the queen... to makes sure she fulfils her end of the bargain," with that Akemi waved her dagger back and forth with a swoosh, "And I'll gather everyone in here to wait for you." The queen interrupted her: "I won't willingly go without my brother... good luck dragging me in your attempted escape. I'd rather die or have you die at the hands of my advisors than leave without him." She snapped

"We've got it," Akemi snapped, rolling her eyes at the white-haired beauty, "We are not animals... we will help you get your bro and meet right here." She turned to Aerwyn. "Be fast, Aer. I don't know how long we can keep eleven mers crammed in this little hole in the wall." With that, Gwylfai gave her directions to the dungeon of the palace and she was off.

The directions were good, but Aerwyn thought she would never have made it up there by wandering alone. There were many turns and spirals of ice that she had to swim up. She felt suffocated and confined swimming up so deep in the ice, the walls of the ice berg becoming thicker and thicker, closing her off from the open ocean. She had just started to panic that she was never going to get to the dungeon, when she came upon the attic of the castle, a large opening with rows of doors on one side. There, guarding the dungeon, was the merjelly that Gwylfai had described. Aerwyn was relieved that Gwylfai had warned her about this, as she was sure she would have passed out from surprise had she not known it was coming. The merjelly was half man, half jellyfish. His large, muscular torso rose out of a skirt of jelly and strong, deadly tentacles, about six feet in length. Accompanying her fear came a strange sense of kinship with him. He was an outsider because of his tentacles, just as she was because of her skin.

"Oh!" Exclaimed Aerwyn, trying to sound surprised and dumb. "Where am I? I got lost in all of those spirals." The merjelly looked at her skeptically for a moment, but must have thought she looked harmless in her flowing robes and purple skin.

"Well, little maid," he said in a gruff voice, "this here is the prison. I don't think it suits your sensibilities to be up here."

He seems harmless, Aerwyn thought. But she remembered Gwylfai's warning. Because they were made with old magic, no longer in use, merjellies were unstable and unpredictable in their violence. She made a quick note of the layout of the jail, and then spoke to distract him. "Are the prisoners so very terrible? Is it a difficult job to keep them in their cells?"

"They are pretty harmless," replied the merjelly. Flattered by her attention, he moved closer.

"Do you mind if I look around" Aerwyn asked, feeling very uncomfortable at the decreasing distance between them. He was cornering her against an ice wall.

"No problem with me," he responded, moving closer. Now he was inches from her. Aerwyn tried to calm her panicking brain. She felt around the ice wall behind her. Her hand latched on to a piece of ice, and she gently disengaged it from the wall. To cover the noise of the ice breaking, she spoke over it.

"Uh, so what are your job duties," she asked.

"Just to keep little mers like yourself safe," he replied.

He thinks I'm not a threat, she thought. This is the one time it pays to be not taken seriously, she noted to herself as her heart was racing. He was so close to her now that she could feel the bubbles coming out of his gills. What is he going to do? she thought momentarily, but she didn't want to know. The merjelly reached his hand up, as if to touch her face, and she seized her opportunity. Before the merjelly could react, Aerwyn slammed the ice chunk into his head with all of her strength. He slumped over immediately and sank to the floor.

She got to work fast, calling out "Sir!? Sir?! Prince Gwylin?!" A few moans came out of the cages. Just as Aerwyn thought this might take a while to locate the prince, a hand shot out of a cell near the end of the row on the left. She swam up to it. That must be Gwylin, she thought as she peered in. He looked exactly like his sister, but his long hair was in one braid, instead of loose about his shoulders. She unlocked the cell door and quickly explained what was going on. "You're leaving the castle with your sister. We need the Eldoris." Gwylin, although visibly malnourished and weak, was mentally sharp. He took in what Aerwyn was saying instantly, and he swam back into the cell to put a silver cuff sporting a small chambered nautilus shell, hidden under a pile of ice, around his wrist. As he was doing so, Aerwyn took a better look at him and stifled a gasp. His whole body was covered in bruises and gashes, and he was incredibly skinny. What had they been doing to him up here? When he came to the opening of the cell, Aerwyn offered him her arm. "Come here sir," she said with sympathy for his ruined body, "I'll help you get down from here."

The going was slow down the spirals as Gwylin had trouble swimming on his own. It wasn't long before Aerwyn heard a noise above her. It was the merjelly, grumbling and bouncing down the ice tube clumsily. Aerwyn's body prickled with fear, and she tried to pick up speed. It was such slow going with Gwylin, and she was practically dragging him down the tube of ice as it was. I could leave him here, she thought. She pushed that thought out of her mind.

She heard movement in the tunnel ahead of her. They were going to be trapped between two enemy mers. Her mind raced, trying to come up with an explanation. She dropped onto an opening, and the merjelly, who had gained a lot of ground, slid in right after her. His eyes were red, and his whole body was shaking with rage. Aerwyn grabbed at Gwylin and pushed him behind her. The merjelly descended on her, grinning with rage from ear to ear.

"There is no escaping me now, little maid," he hissed.

Aerwyn noticed that his teeth had been sharpened into points. She had an out of body moment where she wondered if he ate from his mouth or from where his tentacles sprouted. She reached around behind her, scraping at the ice, trying again to grab something sharp. Nothing was coming off. He descended on her, laughing now. His hand was reaching for her waist. While she screamed on the inside, she braced herself against the wall, ready to head butt him. She would rather die trying to fend him off than let him fulfil his lecherous purpose. Then, an inch from her body, he slumped to the ground, an arrow in his back. Aerwyn looked up. It was Fenn.

"It seems like I'm always rescuing you from jellyfish," he said with a grim smile that had a hint of the earlier warmth in it.

"I could have kept him off." Aerwyn joked feebly, but smiled gratefully at him. Relief spread over her body from her head to the tip of her tail. Something else warmed her from the inside as well, but she shook it off. "Let's get out of here," she said, and the mers each put one arm of Gwylin over their shoulders and dragged him the rest of the way down the tube. Aerwyn glanced over at Fenn, his muscular body tensed from holding up the prince, his face set in its usual serious determination.

When they arrived at the alcove, no one was there. Not having discussed a back-up plan, Aerwyn and Fenn decided they should try to at least get outside the castle walls before anyone came looking for them. The back entrance was guard less, and as soon as they were outside, she could see why. The guards were bound and gagged, and the group was waiting with anxiety. As soon as they made it to the group, Gwylfai rushed to her brother and embraced him. Both had tears in their eyes.

"Where's Puakai?!" Fenn whisper yelled to the group as the all gathered together.

"She said she saw something yesterday... that she had an exit plan. She left" replied Ula.

"And you guys let her go alone!?" Fenn whispered in a rage.

"She said it was our best chances, mate. That no one would suspect her alone. We're out of options here," replied Lachlan sheepishly.

Aerwyn reached out to touch Fenn's arm, "I'm sure she is okay," she said quietly, "she's very smart and quick your sister."

Fenn turned to Aerwyn, his eyes stormy, "It's you again, you every time... distracting me from protecting my sister. Take care of yourself next time Aerwyn," he lashed out quietly, so no one else could hear him.

"I didn't need your help! I was handling that situation just fine," snapped Aerwyn.

"It sure seemed that way," he retorted sarcastically. Under his breath he muttered, "This is why I can't be distracted," and he swam off. The warm feelings Aerwyn felt at the sight of him in the tunnel disappeared.

Fenn's anxiety was short-lived. Lachlan spotted Puakai coming from the stables, a small figure on top of a speckled arctic skate, that looked very much like the stingrays and skates of Biscay. She was leading a pack of saddled skates by a tether. As she pulled up, Fenn hopped on the saddle behind her. "Quick!" Earendil said, and Aerwyn hopped on a smaller skate. Then, under the worried eyes of the bound guards, the skates glided through the water on their flat wings, away from the castle and out of Is.

Chapter 19: On the Waves Again

At Gwylfai's insistence, they rode for two days without stopping. Aerwyn and the others tied themselves to the saddles on the skates, so that, when they nodded off, they did not fall off. In addition to riding hard without stops, Earendil changed their course. He had told the Arcticana advisors that the group was headed to the Indian Ocean next. He changed the plan so that now they would travel down the west side of the Pacific Ocean, thousands of leagues from his home on the east side, and down to the Southern Ocean. When he was speaking about this change of plans, turned backward on his skate to face the group, Aerwyn could not hold back her tears and had to put her head down on the back of her speckled skate to let her tears flow. She didn't even know that the plan was to pass back through Atlantica, but now that she knew that she wouldn't be, it was all she wanted. She missed Coventina very much.

During the two days of travel on the arctic skates, the party got to know Gwylfai and Gwylin better. Gwylfai described the events that led up to the current regime of advisors. Her mother had died a six months ago, and the advisors, who had been posturing for a long time under her mother's nose, took action. They immediately separated the twins. They told the mers of Arcticana that Gwylin was ill, but really they were keeping him in the dungeons. They tortured him whenever Gwylfai did not do as they demanded. They told the mers of Arcticana that Gwylfai had been struck mute by the grief from her mother's death. If she spoke, they would devise some new and terrible harm for Gwylin. So, she was silent.

One time, with the help of Linny, the attendant who had dressed Aerwyn for the ball, Gwylfai attempted to break her brother out of his cell. That had only landed her brother more beatings. One of the other attendants Gwylfai had trusted had been paid a great sum to report on her. That was the last time she trusted anyone but Linny. She had been biding her time, looking for the best opening for escape when the travelers in search of the Eldoris had arrived. She hopped on the opportunity. It was her intention to return to her city, oust the advisors, and rule it with the support of the other tribes.

Gwylfai's opinion was that the advisors wouldn't necessarily want her back for her own safety, but to continue the control over the ruler that they had prior. She thought they would stop at nothing in order to get her back. Her people wanted a queen and had been growing antsy with the current situation where their queen was a silent figurehead. When she spoke about this, Gwylfai's beautiful silver pale face and slanted radiant green eyes had a shadow of shame pass over them. "I will return to my home to lead my people the right way." She said. "Once we are finished reuniting the Five, I will find a way back."

When she said this, Fenn nodded his head in agreement and said "I'll help, any way I can." Lachlan and Figgs joined this pledge quickly. Akemi rolled her eyes and looked at Ula, and Ula looked with dagger eyes at Lachlan. Aerwyn felt the pit in her stomach get a little heavier. Shortly after this pledge of assistance, Ula sidled up to Lachlan, as if to remind him of her presence. It worked for Ula, as it always did. Lachlan followed her like a sad seahorse. When she asserted herself, she got what she wanted.

They traveled quickly and efficiently on the backs of the skates. They had lost their conch shell carriage back in Arcticana and now had to forage and hunt for food. They had their satchels from the belongings they rescued from their rooms, so they were able to bed down comfortably each night. As soon as they stopped for the first time, after nearly 48 hours of travel, Aerwyn immediately changed out of the sheer shirt. She stuffed the silky souvenir from the ball deep into her satchel. She braided her loose black hair into three long braids over her head and down her back. She felt more like her. Gwylfai appeared to not notice the discomfort of traveling with a large cape flapping around her, and elegantly sat atop of her shark with her translucent fur lined cape, giant diamonds, and flowing hair, looking fabulous and leaving nothing to the imagination. The first night, Aerwyn squeezed in Ula's hammock with her, and gave Gwylfai and Gwylin hers. So far Gwylin had barely said a word, but he offered Aerwyn a grateful warm smile whenever she looked his way.

Fenn also barely spoke to Aerwyn, and he definitely wasn't smiling at her. This came in sharp contrast because Aerwyn could not help but look at him. She didn't know how she ever thought he wasn't handsome. He was long and lean, and his magnum red hair and firm jaw and nose seemed to fit his strong and secretly caring personality perfectly. She could not forget that pushing-pulling sensation of being near him, and she desired to have it again. But Fenn seemed to have forgotten all about that tension filled dance and warm conversation following it.

Even though she was exhausted at night, she couldn't help her mind coming back to him when it was quiet and the rest were sleeping. Most of all, he had stirred something in her when he recognized that part in her that she knew was a good part, but never could make it stand out. That part where she tried to bring people together. She sighed when she thought about this. It was pretty brave to be nice to people all the time. To give them the benefit of the doubt, or be polite to those she disliked… that took some energy. Fenn had articulated that when he said she held the group together. She felt like no one but Coventina, not even Ula, had seen value in that part of her before. But he also still thought of her as a burden apparently, which stung.

"Ula," she whispered to the lump next to her in the hammock, "are you asleep?"

"Not anymore," Ula muttered.

"What am I good at Ula?" she asked

Ula rolled over to face, "Oh Aer, you're good at so many things. You're a fast swimmer… you know a lot about humans… you're funny… Is that Fenn thing getting to you still?"

"A little. Maybe. But it is more of like, what am I going to do after this… like for a career?"

"Like I told you, you can be my personal advisor! You'll always have a job."

Aerwyn laughed, but it was more out of habit than anything, "thanks Ula."

She rolled over, she didn't really want to do that. She wanted to do her own thing--something she was good at.

They traveled on the backs of the whale sharks for just five days before they had to cross over the Aleutian trench, the 25,000 fins deep abyss that Aerwyn had learned about during her history classes. Here, Earendil wanted to take a detour.

Chapter 20: In the Deep

The mers set up their camp for the night a few tails away from the edge in a spacious cave, surrounded by corals of vibrant reds and oranges and protected from sight by dense yellow sea grass. The cave had clearly been used as shelter before. There were small hieroglyphs, of a language Aerwyn did not recognize, carved into the wall. Earendil studied them closely.

During a meager dinner of fish and some unrecognizable greens that Gwylin foraged, Earendil announced that he would be descending into The Deep for a second time the next day. He instructed the group to stay in the cave for a few days, and that if he wasn't back up in three days, to come looking for him. When questioned why he needed to take this detour, he held up his hand, as if to stop the questioning, but still answered the questions, albeit vaguely. He needed more information about the Eldoris, and the information was in the trench. He picked Akemi and, to everyone's surprise, Aerwyn, to accompany him. When Aerwyn heard this, a feeling of dread passed over her. Her last experience in The Deep was less than pleasant.

After they were finished eating, the mers were more quiet than usual. Fenn stormed around, trying to organize their belongings for more longevity in the cave. That took about five minutes, since they really had nothing. Then he went out and lurked around the tethered skates. He had asked Earendil to go too, and Earendil refused. Lachlan also was miffed that he hadn't been asked to join the task. Figgs and Folander on the other hand seemed incredibly relieved to get a day off and spent the evening quietly ribbing each other.

"Hey, remember that time you were on your first combing expedition?" Folander asked his younger brother. "You thought that dead bird was a fish?"

"I don't know what you are talking about," replied Figgs with feigned ignorance.

"Yeah, yeah. You brought it to the commander, convinced you had made some discovery of a large finned fish with… what did you call the feathers? Oh right, hairy scales."

Figgs punched his brother in the arm. "Well, dearest brother, do you remember the time you met your future wife? And she asked me to Poseidon's dance and not you?" It was Folander's turn to punch his brother.

Aerwyn's braids had come undone due to the high speeds the skates had reached. While she listened to the two brothers, she brushed out her black strands with her fingers and braided them back into three braids over her head and down her back.

As she was finishing the third braid, Fenn came up to her, looking sullen. He sat next to her for a moment without saying anything. Confused, Aerwyn continued on with her braid and looked at him, trying to look indifferent, the hurt of his words still stinging.

"Be careful down there Aerwyn. I don't know what Earendil is up to but... well... I think he puts this whole Eldoris thing above any mer's life. Right or wrong, I don't know yet... but if the chances are high it will succeed... anyway. Just keep that in mind. And," he paused for a second, as if hesitant to say the next part, "please come back." He looked at her for a long moment, his jaw firm but his eyes soft.

Taken aback, Aerwyn thought, this must be his apology for getting mad about the merjelly. Not knowing how to respond to this most recent mood swing, she joked, "I think it is the trench that has to look out for me." Fenn's face set back to its usually sternness, and he swam off. Ugh, Aerwyn thought, why couldn't I just say something normal? Like let him know that I accept his apology? She sat there in regret and watched as Gwylfai sidled up beside Fenn, white hair flowing and eyes glimmering. Aerwyn felt the unfamiliar twang of jealousy in her chest.

Aerwyn was awoken by Earendil before the beams of sun had reached their depths. Ula sleepily wished her good luck. She grabbed her satchel, which contained barely two days of provisions. Figgs and Folander had a hard time finding any substance of fish, so her bag was packed with several small fry. Her stomach was already grumbling. She hoisted the satchel onto her back and inhaled through her gills deeply. Here goes, she thought.

They quickly lost all light. They had left their angler fish back at the castle in Is in their rush to leave. So, they hugged the wall as they descended into the trench. This was the easiest way to stay protected and not get lost in the deep abyss. The going was slow, and the trio didn't speak much. Soon their way was lit by wild angler fish, flitting this way and that, providing short moments of sight. These angler fish were not bred in captivity and had the ugly, lumpy look of the dark bred creatures that Aerwyn had heard about in her science classes. The wild anglers wanted nothing to do with the mers and swam away quickly, but not before alighting for a moment the sheer rock walls of the trench and the blackness below.

Aerwyn started to become uncomfortable with the silence, so she asked Earendil more about what they were doing: "Mr. um Earendil, what exactly are we doing in this trench" and, to seem less pushy "so that I can, you know, keep my eyes out better."

"Hmmm" replied Earendil, not taking his gaze away from the direction they were headed, "well, I guess there is no hiding it. I need to speak with Callan, the last Vodianoi. Legend has it that he receded here at the time of the Five, to stay safe from their magic eradication."

Both Akemi and Aerwyn had a sharp intake of breath take them by surprise. Akemi recovered first. "Wait, Earendil, there are still Vodianoi alive? The water spirits that would drown any human in its path?"

"Hmmm. Well, Akemi, yes. But those legends are only half true. The Vodianoi were like me and the other mermagicians. They knew the old magic, and they practiced it. They didn't seek out humans to drown per se, but they were less… patient… than some of us other magic users. If a human got near a Vodianoi settlement, that human would draw its last breaths." Earendil paused for a moment as he navigated around a rock sticking out from the cliff. "But you see," he continued, almost sadly "when the Five came together, they put regulations on magic. For our safety, they said. And the Vodianoi wouldn't have it. Us mermagicians, we were used to living with the regular mers… and the threat of the humans was so strong. My ancestors would do anything they thought would help protect our people, including using magic only to heal, as the Five's law required. The Vodianoi were not so complacent. They receded deeper and deeper into the oceans to escape the regulation. And the Five... they ordered the Vodianoi destroyed if ever encountered. Now, I believe, there is only one left. He lives in this trench with his wife, a Rusalaka named Marna. They are the last of those who know any of the old magic. I think..." he paused for a moment, as if hesitating to tell them the next part "that they will know how to unite the Eldoris."

Aerwyn was shocked. They were going to see a Vodianoi? She thought they were all gone! That's what she had been told in her history class at least. All she really knew about Vodianoi was that they were half mer half sea. As for Rusalaka, she had only heard the horror stories that Coventina had told her about mers with legs luring men in from the sea to drown them. She put her hand at her hip where here dagger was. Not that it will help me much, she thought with a shiver. Akemi seemed equally as taken aback, and remained quiet for a long time.

Aerwyn's mind churned over the information, and eventually she couldn't help herself from asking Earendil "So, if these two know how to unite the Eldoris… was the plan to pass this way the whole time, and not stop back at Atlantica?"

Earendil looked kindly at her, which was weird for him. "It was Aerwyn. You don't know who you can trust. Even those with the best intentions can ruin your plans."

That stuck with Aerwyn for the next hour or so. Does he mean me? If I was a plan ruiner, why would he pick me to come down here then? Why would he tell me that? Did he mean someone else? Ula? Fenn or Lachlan? They had been so helpful so far. Her mind churned his statement around over and over. She tried tell herself to stop obsessing about that comment and tuck it away for later. It kept popping up though. Who did he mean?

They swam for seven hours exactly, with no stops, before Earendil indicated that it was time to rest. They pulled out their food and ate ravenously. Then, rather than going down further, they turned left. As they passed by the trench wall, electric eels flitted in and out of the cliff side next to them. Their slithering bodies and dangerous tails creeped Aerwyn out, and she stayed as far away from them as possible. Then, suddenly, Earendil halted. "We are here" he whispered.

Chapter 21: The Vodianoi

Earendil slipped into the wall of the trench. One moment he was hovering along the side, and the next moment he was gone. Aerwyn and Akemi tentatively approached the space where he had disappeared. There was a long narrow crack in the wall. Aerwyn looked at Akemi, who shrugged and slipped in the crack behind Earendil. Aerwyn took a big gulp of water, and slipped in behind her. Immediately the crack opened up into a large domed cave with coral growing out of every side, including the ceiling. Aerwyn wondered how the coral could grow without light from the surface or nutrients. It's the old magic, she thought. The coral garden was lit from an undiscoverable source. It was well cared for, and it was clear that someone lived here.

"Who enters?!" A creaky voice demanded from the depths of the cave.

"Earendil, mermagician for the Pacificanas, Akemi, comber of Pacificana, and Aerwyn, granddaughter of mermagician Coventina and student of Atlantica." Projected Earendil confidently. "We are here in peace, seeking knowledge only."

From the back of the cave, something started to move slowly out of the shadows. At first Aerwyn could make out nothing more than the form of a mer emerging from the darkness. As it got closer, and moved into the light of the angler fish, she made out a face that looked like a freshwater amphibian, with wide lips and big red eyes. Callan had green slimy hair and a beard that grew to his waist in a scraggly mess. She couldn't tell where beard ended and tail began for his body was covered in algae and muck, as if he had been lying in a pit of slime for years and never bothered to scrub himself.

Earendil bowed, which made Aerwyn feel uncomfortable-- how powerful is this guy that Earendil, the great mermagician, has to bow, she wondered. She awkwardly followed his lead. "Great Callan, what a wonder it is to see you and feel the old magic in the air." Earendil started. Aerwyn just now noticed that Earendil had taken the time to braid his long white hair, as well as scrub some of the travelers scum off of his tail. "As you can tell, we are mers of different tribes. We also have been joined by two mers from Arcticana. It is with this kinship that we seek your most gracious assistance."

Aerwyn was caught off guard. Even when he had presented their case to the advisors of Atlantica and Arcticana, Earendil had not been so obsequious.

Callan replied in his creaky voice and looked at Aerwyn when he spoke: "Rare. Rare indeed." His red eyes bore into Aerwyn. "What's this one?" He asked, his eyes pointing at her.

Earendil spoke: "her grandmother," and he coughed, "raised her from a child. But, she comes from Atlantica."

Callan looked back at Aerwyn. "So, I see" he replied. "Come in, come in then. It has been many years since Marna and I have had guests. Please excuse the mess." He floated back into the depths of the cave, looking back only once to beckon the mers to follow him.

They swam through a small opening at the back of the cave, which opened up to another, smaller cave. It was a room of a home, but clearly it was not guest ready. Everything was covered in algae. The center of the room bore a magnificent human chandelier, but it was green with slime and only one orb had an angler fish in it. There was an opening off to the side, through which Aerwyn could see algae covered hammocks. The opening off to the other side appeared to lead to a kitchen.

When Aerwyn's eyes adjusted to the dim light, she saw Marna, who was sitting in a coral chair in the back of the room. She gasped, Marna, had legs. The legends about Rusalaka were true. She had never seen legs before, and she subtly wiggled her own tail thinking about what it must feel like to have it split into two independent parts. She didn't take her eyes off of the legs until Marna got up and swam to meet the guests, at which time Aerwyn's manners returned to her.

"Greetings," she said in a silky ancient voice that reminded Aerwyn of Coventina, but without the warmth. "Welcome to our home. I'm supposing you are weary, and you are wanting nourishment." Before the mers could object, she whisked herself away through the door to the kitchen, and Aerwyn was given a view of the swimming legs in motion. She was thrilled at seeing real legs in person.

They sat in silence for a few moments. Aerwyn was just wondering whether they were going to wait like this while Marna prepared a full meal, and how uncomfortable that would be, when Marna gracefully whisked back into the room with a platter full of steaming hot foods. Aerwyn looked with confusion at Akemi, and Akemi mouthed silently "magic" to her. "While we talk, let's eat" said Callan.

Then, Earendil launched into the tale of how the Pacificanas came to Atlantica, how both tribes sent members to Arcticana, and how, so far, they had recruited royalty from each tribe. He described with great passion his hope to unite the Eldoris in order to commune with the humans to save the oceans. Callan listened silently, his hands folded lightly in front of him. Marna, on the other hand, was staring at Aerwyn. Even when Aerwyn made eye contact with her, the Rusalaka maintained her inquisitive gaze. She's got legs! Thought Aerwyn. My hair and skin cannot possibly be that shocking to her--what's her issue?

After Earendil brought Callan up to speed on how they had made it to the trench, and who was in their little environmentalist band, Earendil asked another question that confused Aerwyn. He played with his long white beard for a moment, as if pondering whether to ask at all. "I'm also wondering about the Changed. Can they do anything to help unite the Eldoris? To maybe lessen any…. Risk… to the royal blood?"

Callan looked thoughtfully at Earendil, and it took him a long time to answer. His flakey, dry voice seemed unused to long discourse, and he had to stop several times to refresh himself with dulse wine as he related his wisdom of the Eldoris. He asked whether the band had all female leaders, which Earendil confirmed. He asked if we for sure had all of the Eldoris, which Earendil also confirmed. This made the necklace burn around Aerwyn's neck, but she had become pretty good at hiding that. Marna seemed to notice though. She nodded just slightly at Aerwyn.

"Earendil the environmentalist, this is a bold thing that you are doing. I know there are many out there, including myself who hoped the days of communing with the humans were over. You expose yourself and all of the oceans' mers to their thoughtless experiments and exhibitions." He paused for several seconds and continued sadly "but, it doesn't matter if I think you are right to seek this course. Information is information. I have no right to withhold my information from you." He scooped a pile of orange mush into his froglike mouth, and continued, unconcerned that they could see the contents of his mouth. "We are going to all die soon anyway. There is barely enough food now, I don't know what will happen in the next 100 years. I commend you for that. I also commend your comrades. If the female royalty, and the spell requires they are female, from the five tribes are strong enough, I believe they may survive the effort. The spell is not meant to kill… but it can, especially if a mer is not full grown and able to take the exertion. The presence of a Changed can weaken that barrier between the ocean and the land, since the changed have lived on both and have a liminal existence about them. There used to be a Changed in Arcticana who would consistently go to the surface and assist humans stuck in the ice bergs, but he was imprisoned by the leaders there after the meeting of the Five. But, I am getting off topic, if you will follow me, I can show you my research on the matter, and what I believe will work to break the spell of the Five." and with that, he put his food down, got up, and beckoned Earendil to join him. Aerwyn and Akemi looked questioningly at Earendil, to see if they wanted them to join, Akemi grasping hard at the knife on her waist. He shook his head slightly. So, the two mers turned back to their meals.

"Err… Marna" said Akemi, who had noticed that she was staring at Aerwyn, "thank you for your hospitality mate, err, madam."

Marna turned to Akemi, "You're most welcome," she said in her smooth archaic voice. She stared at them unflinchingly.

"I would warn you mers about these mermen. Their risk is not as great. They are not the ones who are putting themselves at risk by attempting this spell." She paused for a moment, slowly turning her gaze from Aerwyn to Akemi and then back again. "Everything will change. Some good, much bad." The three heard Earendil and Callan swimming back into the room and Marna's voice dropped "Go back to your homes. Protect yourselves. The life of a Changed is no life. Look at me if you don't believe me" she whispered fiercely. This took both of the merwomen aback. She then straightened herself and was completely composed once Callan reentered the room.

As the mers took their leave of the Vodianoi and the Rusalaka, they were invited to stay the night. Earendil politely refused, indicating that they had a tight schedule to keep. Aerwyn could have kissed him. She wanted to get away from those creepy mer-creatures who lived in a world that time had passed by as soon as possible. She didn't even want to think about sleeping in one of their slimy green hammocks. They bade farewell, Marna never moving her eyes from Aerwyn, and made their way out of the cave and back up the side of the trench.

Chapter 22: On the Backs of Skates

It took Aerwyn the entire trip back to the rim of the trench to shake the weird feelings that attached to her during their meal with Callan and Marna. By the time she made it to the top, she had been able to mostly push them out of her mind, but she still felt strange about the whole thing. She mulled over what the two had said. The spell to break the barrier between the ocean and the land was not meant to kill those who cast it, but it could. On the swim back to the group, Earendil had sworn she and Akemi to silence on the matter, telling them that he would never let anyone die, and that the safety of the royalty depended on their ignorance of the matter. Aerwyn didn't know how much she understood of this second part. However, the more she saw of the ocean beyond her rocky home in Biscay, the more she understood the need to protect the oceans. The dwindling number of mers, the scarcity of fish to eat and greens to gather, that horrible oil pit between the Norwegian sea and the Greenland Sea--it all came together for her now. So she made the promise to Earendil not to tell, trusting his judgment.

The other mers were waiting anxiously for them when they returned, tired and hungry. Aerwyn's heart warmed at the sight of the group, melded from three tribes, coming together into their rag tag band. Ula gave her the biggest hug of all, and whispered how much she missed her, which made Aerwyn feel warmer, since Ula rarely expressed those feelings that Aerwyn knew they shared. Lachlan, Figgs, Folander, and Puakai also gave her big hugs. Gwylfai and Gwylin smiled at her politely. Fenn came up last. Aerwyn felt minnows swimming inside of her as he approached. She gave him a big smile, but he just hovered in front of her, flicking his tail nervously. "Glad you're back" he said and he reached out and awkwardly patted her arm. Aerwyn didn't know what to do, so she said "me too."

Early the next morning they mounted the skates, who were restless after being tethered for two days, and rode across the trench. The cold water from The Deep passed over their fins, and it made Aerwyn glad she was back up to the sea floor. The skates adeptly navigated though the mountains on the other side of the trench. Aerwyn could see why they hadn't traveled this way before. While it was nice to not have to swim all day, this took an entirely different muscle group to hold on to the skates, and the force of the water pummeling against her body was exhausting. Her arms and back were weak and sore from hanging onto her ride's harness for hours at a time. The only rope that they had went to tying Puakai and Gwylin, who was still weak from his injuries, to the skates. Everyone else had to hold on as they rushed through the water. As such, even though they were going faster, they had to take many more breaks than if they were swimming. Finn and Folander had been prize winning eel riders at the Brine Festival, so they were comfortably riding along and enjoying themselves.

As she rode, Aerwyn became less and less confident of the value of her promise to Earendil. What if something did happen to Ula, and she had the power to warn her all along? The farther they got from the mystic trench, the more Aerwyn found that she needed to share what the Vodianoi had said. Earendil's request for secrecy unsettled her. She reasoned that she should at least tell her best friend, and that Akemi could use her own judgment as to telling her tribe.

When they set up camp that night, Aerwyn was able to find a way to get alone time with Ula under the guise of gathering wakame from a nearby patch for their dinner. The two friends were swimming over the patch, plucking the strands of wakame from sea floor and placing them into their satchels when Aerwyn drew a deep breath and broke her promise. "Ula, I must tell you about what actually happened with Callan and Marna," she said.

Ula stopped picking and swam upright. Her silence inviting Aerwyn to continue.

"Callan, he said that uniting the Eldoris could really harm the mers involved in the process. He said that the risk wasn't great to healthy mers, but that there was still risk. He then went on about the Changed, whatever that is, and how the Changed makes the process easier. So, like I don't know if we are going to look for a Changed or not?" Ula nodded silently, and Aerwyn continued, "Then Earendil spoke to Callan in private... so I don't know what he said there. But then there was Marna. She totally creeped me out with her legs. But she said that everything will change. I think she said some good and much bad. So, I don't know... I wanted you to know that."

Ula didn't seem shocked by what the Vodianoi and Rusalaka had told Aerwyn. "Thanks for telling me that, Aer," she responded calmly.

"Aren't you worried?" asked Aerwyn.

"I am worried. I don't want to get hurt or die or anything like that. But my mom did tell me that there could be a risk... she actually offered to go herself instead."

"What?" Aerwyn asked, shocked. "Ulayn, I'm sorry, Queen Ulayn offered to go instead?"

"Yeah," Ula replied, "But I wanted to go. I've been itching to do something other than learn about Biscay policies." She grabbed Aerwyn's hand, "And I'm glad I did! Look what we have seen Aerwyn. This has to be done." Ula grabbed her friend's hand as they sat together on the bed of wakame.

"I mean, I agree… but it is not me who has to risk her life." Aerwyn responded with admiration for her friend. A thought burst into her mind, that might help her friend stay a little bit safer. The Eldoris. Coventina trusted me with this, she thought, this is my judgment call. She took a deep breath, "You've got a fake," she said, fingering her coral necklace.

Ula was silent for a second, processing what her friend told her, and then she exclaimed "That's why you went back into that jellyfish swarm!" She grabbed the crown off of her head and looked at it. "Good to know… I'm not going to risk my life trying to protect this fake Eldoris. Does Earendil know?"

"I don't think so," said Aerwyn. "I don't think he would have brought me to Callan knowing I had such a valuable item. Who knows whether Callan would have stolen it. He did not seem super supportive of the whole thing. Besides, Coventina told me to keep it a secret right up until we need it. I don't think she entirely trusted Earendil," continued Aerwyn. She got a cramp in her heart at that moment, thinking of her savvy grandmer.

Ula could tell, from the change of Aerwyn's tone, that she was missing her grandmer. "Aw, Aer," she said, draping her arm around her friend, "too bad your grandmer isn't a total sea witch like my mom… then you might miss her less." The talk of Ulayn and making fun of her sternness brought the mers back to their days in Biscay, lounging in the library, swimming in races, and leading an easier existence. They allowed themselves to take a break from the seriousness of the Eldoris and took a swim down memory lane. They reminisced together for over an hour in the bed of wakame, until they heard Folander calling for them.

"Whoops!" exclaimed Ula, laughing unapologetically and frantically gathering the vegetable. "I hope they weren't waiting on us to eat." This hour did a world of good for both friends. They felt refreshed and themselves again. The anger that Aerwyn felt after their escape from Is had vanished.

The next few days passed quickly, and Aerwyn had a second to take stock of some things she didn't talk to Ula about, like what happened with Fenn at the ball and that push pull she felt. Did he feel it too? Ever since the ball, he barely looked at her. To make matters more confusing, both he and Figgs started lingering around the beautiful Gwylfai, who still didn't seem to care about the rough road enough to put on a shirt. This was something both Aerwyn and Ula found annoying, considering the number of sarcastic looks they shared when she would swim by.

Fenn had revealed the depth of his love and loyalty towards his sister when they danced at the ball. Aerwyn knew she had misjudged his stormy and cold exterior. But he hadn't shown that part of him again. She also wondered if she should rely on Akemi to tell the Pacificanas about the risks of uniting the Eldoris. Was Fenn's talk of risk just about the journey? Or did he know more? And was Akemi more loyal to Earendil, as his right-hand mer, than to her princess?

On one evening, while Aerwyn's brain was cycling through these thoughts for the millionth time, Lachlan spotted a pod of blue whales, swimming up towards the surface and frolicking in the waves amongst the late day sun rays. They were the largest creatures that Aerwyn had ever seen. They were as graceful as they were large, and their sad echoing songs made Aerwyn think of times past, when the ocean filled with creatures such as these. Watching them made Aerwyn yearn for the uniting of the Eldoris and a return to a time when they could live communally with the creatures of the sea, without fear for their safety. The group kept their distance from the whales, because it had been many years since the mers and whales had lived together, and they had to move on.

It took them one week to make it to the seat of the Southern Ocean. When they arrived, it was immediately apparent that something was off. The city was not what Aerwyn had expected. The legendary sand castles towering leagues above the sea floor were nowhere to be seen. In their place were stone hovels and piles of sand.

Chapter 23: The Golden Ocean

At the Academy, Aerwyn had studied all five oceans in depth. Thus far, Arcticana had more than exceeded her expectations with its grandeur and splendor. The iceberg castle and surrounding dwellings carved into spires of ice and rock had been shocking to the mer who came from a settlement of natural caves. It was far wealthier and far more populated than Atlantica. The Southern Ocean on the other hand did not live up to the descriptions she had been taught. She had heard of monstrous sand castles, shooting one hundred tails up into the ocean. The city of Lazarev, the seat of the Southern Ocean, was known for its mining and metal-making industry. Many of the metal works, weapons, jewelry, and tools in Atlantica had come originally, in some form or other, from trade with the Southerns back before each tribe had sunk into itself. Aerwyn had heard tales of the traditional penguin dish, served at holidays and special gatherings, that tasted like no fish you had ever tasted. What Aerwyn saw instead was a city in crumbles.

The whole party stopped short and was silent. They had tethered the skates and Lachlan was leading them at the rear of the group. Aerwyn wondered if anyone even lived here anymore. Fenn swam up next to Aerwyn, and she could hear him breathing through his gills. She wanted to grab his hand.

Instead, she just chanced a look at him. His face was firm and determined. This would all be for nothing if there was no longer a Southern tribe, and she wondered if she didn't see a bit of relief on Fenn's face as well. He looked back at her, and for a moment, his relief, mixed with guilt, shown in his eyes. Then, to Aerwyn's surprise, he grabbed her hand.

The moment was over as quickly as it had begun as Earendil ushered the group into the ruins. They passed hovel after hovel, with no sign of life. Earendil was calm, but Aerwyn wondered if he was panicking inside. For this to work, they needed a female heir from every tribe, just as Callan had confirmed. As they swam through the abandoned homes, a large pile of broken sand towers and mounds of rocks and sand loomed up in front of them. That must have been the largest castle here, thought Aerwyn, sadly taking in the towers, strewn like sticks on a pile. I wonder what happened? As they neared, Aerwyn saw that there was a lone mer sitting in front of an opening in the pile. Earendil's sigh of relief was audible.

The mer was thin and bedraggled, but he greeted them kindly and without surprise. His tail was the blue color of the Pacificanas, but instead of the flesh colored skin, his skin and short hair were gold. Aerwyn had learned about this too. The Southerns looked very much like their neighbors to the north, the Pacificanas. To distinguish themselves, they rubbed their mined gold lotion all over their bodies and cut their hair short. So, thought Aerwyn, they must still be mining. "Welcome" greeted the sullen mer, as he ushered them quickly inside.

The inside of the pile of ruins was full of relics from a time gone by. As she followed her comrades through the decrepit passageway into the ruins of the former castle, she passed beautiful iron and coral statues of the ancient mer people. They were polished and clean, but many were chipped or missing pieces. Aerwyn saw statues of what appeared to be humans, their legs were covered by cloth tails, covering up their distinguishing feature. This castle is very old, if it still has remnants from when we communed with humans, thought Aerwyn. The hallway was dim, and there were only a few fixtures that were not broken and containing glowing algae. The others, while clean, had holes or cracks that allowed the light source to slowly escape into the room. As such, there was a glowing green fog floating at the very top of the room as the algae spread onto the ceiling.

The passageway took them this way and that, doing what Aerwyn could only imagine was a zig zag pattern inside of the mound of sand. It appeared to be that they were on some makeshift route that connected the still standing parts of the castle. Finally, they made it to a large triangular hall where there were other Southerners there waiting for them. Seated at the very apex of the room was the littlest adult mer Aerwyn had ever seen. She first thought she was a child, but when she looked more closely, she could see the fine lines of middle age on her face. The little mer was wearing the largest crown Aerwyn had ever seen. It showcased all that the Southerners were known for--intricate metal carvings of iron, gold, and silver, large jewels haphazardly stuck on to the various irregular points and patterns. Aerwyn wondered how she could keep her head up.

They were welcomed coolly and requested to make their errand known at once. Earendil, with palpable relief, swam in front of the queen and once again gave his speech about the need for the five tribes to band together to make change. Every time Aerwyn heard it, she shivered a little. She was part of something great. This shiver of excitement always was accompanied by a wave of doubt. What if I don't add up? What if I just mess this whole thing up? She looked at Ula. Ula shivered too, but no wave of self-doubt followed. I wish I was like that, thought Aerwyn. Instead, her anxiety grew one more inch.

While Aerwyn was immersed in these thoughts, she missed the queen's initial response to Earendil. She looked up as the queen was waving her hand dismissively. "Like I said," she snapped curtly, "no thank you."

"But my Queen, you must recons-"

"No. I will never say yes to something as preposterous as this," she replied. "You are all going to get yourselves killed. And then, you are going to leave your tribes to clean up the nasty human mess. No. You will have to do it without me."

"But, we can-" Earendil was interrupted again.

"You may eat here and enjoy our hospitality tonight. I don't want to hear another word about the Eldoris. If I do, you won't be leaving here tomorrow."

Aerwyn drew a deep breath. For the first time, Earendil looked baffled.

Chapter 24: The Meagerest Meal

While the mers hung about awkwardly, unsure of what to do after their rejection, long silver tables on wheels and benches were rolled into the hall. Several well-kept but very skinny mers set the table for twelve. At the queen's insistence, the travelers gathered around, and the queen sat at the head of the table. The servers and finsmen hovered against the back wall, their eyes fixed on the food and emitting a gleam of hunger. When they caught Aerwyn looking at them, they would look away. This food is nothing to covet, she thought. It was merely what they had been eating on their journey, foraged greens, but not enough, and a few small fish. The way the queen invited them to dig in, you would have thought it was Poseidon's Feast.

Aerwyn couldn't help but let her mind drift to Poseidon's Feast back in Biscay as she picked at the food on her plate. It had been since Is that that they all had a good meal other than greens and small fish that were more bones than meat. Poseidon's Feast was her favorite holiday. The whole city was decorated for the occasion. Coventina would dress the front of their home in the wall of the cliff in bright starfish and sea urchins. The inside was filled with floating garlands of bright beads made from coral and colorful shells.

The day started with physical feats in honor of their great protector. Ever since she could remember, Aerwyn enrolled herself in the swimming races. There were others, spear throwing, eel wrestling, and rock hurling, but Aerwyn liked the swimming. She felt like herself when she was hurtling through the water at breakneck speed. She never won. Ula did most times, a few fins ahead of Aerwyn. Aerwyn usually didn't mind. She swam so that she could see how far she could push or how fast she could go. It was about the personal challenge to herself. However, there were times when she would finish and Ula would be there, emerald green hair and fins, congratulating her, that Aerwyn would be jealous of all the advantages that Ula had. As she grew and learned that these thoughts were not useful to her in any way, she could push them out of her mind--most of the time. She had felt so confident about her ability to just be herself back in Biscay. She hadn't even cared about her purpleness for the past few years. Why did that change now? Why did she feel so unworthy to be with this group of travelers? She didn't know what she was doing, sure, or what she added. She had already contributed by saving Puakai several times, but there was a nagging feeling that wasn't enough. She came out of her reverie for a moment, to take in the small blob of plankton pudding she was eating, and her stomach grumbled.

Aerwyn and her grandmer would work for hours together preparing their own little feast. Miniature coral cakes, topped with agar jam, fish puddings, and kelp trifles--their little table barely had room for it all by the time they dug-in. As Aerwyn got older, and had befriended Ula, she and Coventina were invited to the palace for the official feast. The palace was decorated magnificently, hundreds of seahorses with colorful and luminescent algae strings floating from their backs flitted about near the ceiling, piles of food adorned the tables, and a band of shell and horn players made the whole occasion the best day of the year. The mers all had beads and shells in their hair, and wore their best vests or shirts. Ulayn would wear her largest crown, and give gifts of food and supplies to any mer who came asking.

Aerwyn recalled that she had seen Figgs and Folander at that feast on occasion. Their family must have been higher up in Biscay than she had realized just from interacting with the two jocular mers at the Academy. As they got older, Ula would roll her eyes at the same old traditions, wishing for something more, but Aerwyn never felt that way. She loved her home and its traditions. All the mers were together on the day of

Poseidon's Feast, enjoying their time together despite their differences, just like the old times.

When Aerwyn and Coventina started going to the palace for dinner, they kept their tradition alive by making copious amount of desserts that they would eat together when they got home from the palace's festivities. Then, Coventina would open the vent to the geyser, which filled the room with a warmth that even Aerwyn's cold blooded body could just barely register and would regale Aerwyn with tales of their protector, Poseidon, and what adventures he had. She would talk about the days of magic with some wistfulness in her eyes, and Aerwyn would fall asleep in the main room. Rather than moving her, Coventina would camp out in the main room with her. They would wake up the next day, cozy in their living room, with full bellies and a lot of dishes to do. As Aerwyn got older, and fish became scarcer, the feast part of Poseidon's Feast became smaller and less grand. The Atlanticans tried to do the best they could to keep up the other traditions so that the meager feast was less noticeable.

Aerwyn emerged from her memory as the plates were being cleared away. Lachlan, who was sitting next to her, had jabbed her in the ribs. The little queen was addressing her. "I asked my dear, about how you get your skin so purple."

Aerwyn hadn't heard a question like this since she was a young mer. Her contemporaries had been reprimanded by their parents and advised that asking such a question was rude. She felt a pang of offense for an instant. Then, gathering herself, quickly realized it was a reasonable question coming from someone who put so much effort into changing her own appearance. The gold lotion was prolific on her face, and Aerwyn thought she saw a sheen of lotion that had rubbed off from the queen onto the table.

"I uh," Aerwyn started, as she noticed that everyone at the table was looking at her except Ula, who politely was acting like nothing was happening. Or maybe it was because she already knew the story. "I really don't know. My grandmer said that her daughter, my mum, looked this way. She thought maybe it was because she was a mermagician… you know, rainbow colored and all of that… and I got some of the purple from her. My mum… She died giving birth you see. So my grandmer raised me." The faces around the table looked awkwardly away, and the queen looked like the tale disappointed her in some way.

"Ah, mate, that's tough," Lachlan said.

The little queen pushed on, "So that's not from amethyst dust or coal or anything?"

"No, it is not... it is just my skin" Aerwyn replied

"What color was your dad?" The queen asked.

Aerwyn was about to respond that Coventina never spoke of him when, surprisingly, Earendil came to her rescue. "That's enough on that, let the poor mer eat." Aerwyn looked down, her plate had been removed by the finsmen, but was grateful for the interruption.

Earendil launched into a discussion with the queen, and Fenn leaned over the table and whispered to Aerwyn, "Hey, I'm sorry you never knew your mum. I didn't know that." Aerwyn smiled at him gratefully.

The queen rose, to indicate that the meal was done, and said "now that we have feasted to our hearts' content, I will show you the rest of the palace. You will see how good we have it here." Aerwyn was still very hungry and not at all content.

As she led the tour, rambling on about different topics, the queen started on a tangent that made Aerwyn feel uncomfortable. "As you see, we have covered up all of the human statues. Too indecent. Their barbaric legs have no place in our sea. Lazarev was a mers only city even before the uniting of the Five. In fact, it was our great leader, Laz II who was the main instigator of uniting the Five. She did all of the research on the matter and used a lot of our resources here to...

encourage… the other tribes. For years before the uniting of the Five, we opposed assisting humans, as well as human assistance. We had the right of it, you see. The Five confirmed that."

Apparently unable to help herself, Akemi interjected, "But yeah, don't you think the humans would be better this time? Like, they need the ocean too. They know that now… before… when they hadn't explored all of the earth land yet… it was different. I mean, they did take us for granted then. But now, the world is smaller… and more connected. Don't you think we should be a part of that?"

"Of course not. Why expose ourselves to those grotesque land monsters? They haven't changed. And," she stressed, waving her hand at the decrepit lounge room she was showing them, "As you can see, we need no assistance. We are completely content here."

Akemi looked as if she was going to argue with the queen, but a sharp look from Earendil silenced her. His eyes seemed to say that there was no hope in convincing her, so stop trying.

The tour lasted about ten more minutes. By the end of it, all of the mers had sore tongues from biting them when the queen made offensive comments about the barbaric land monsters.

The tour ended at a large, bare room at the very back of the dilapidated castle.

The queen said, "Unfortunately, this is all we have at the moment for you. We have several other very important guests this evening, who are all using our other, more luxurious spare rooms." With that, she closed the door on the group. They all looked at each other in disbelief.

"Does she actually think we buy that they are doing well here?" asked Puakai.

"Yeah no kidding" replied Ula, as she flopped down next to the little princess. "Like, we ate the same meal she did... we haven't seen any other guests... what is she thinking?"

"Denial is a strong and powerful force," said Earendil quietly, as he swam off to the corner to speak with Akemi.

"Yeah it is," replied Lachlan, as he threw his satchel on the pile of satchels that started to form. "Before I left Pacificana, I was just a dudemer, scavenging the seas with the other combers. Looking for the next meal and telling myself I didn't need to do more. This guy," he gestured to Fenn, "he was the one who made me feel guilty. That I had some sort of obligation to use my combing skills to help Pacificana. I was in denial though even then, because I knew change would be really hard. I didn't want to do it." He put his arm around Fenn,

"But, this stone-faced magnum-headed pal changed my mind… using little words, mind you." The little group that had formed laughed at this. Fenn grimaced but didn't push his friend away.

Gwylfai saddled up to the group, flicking her flowing white hair behind her, "What is this I hear about Fenn? Not a man of many words?" She sat next to Fenn. "I must say, I would say I disagree with that. You have talked to me quite a bit, about all sorts of wonderful things." With that, she linked her arm in his. Fenn immediately tensed up his body and looked uncomfortable; but, as Aerwyn noted and would later replay over and over, he didn't move, and he didn't say no.

Lachlan gave his friend a quizzical look and quickly moved on with his story, which mainly included how he met Earendil, and, since Earendil was preoccupied with Akemi in the other end of the room, his first impressions of the weird mermagician. As Lachlan was describing his first meeting with Earendil, Earendil had been holding a blow fish in one hand and trying to make it deflate in an attempt to propel the shell he was sitting on, the mermagician joined the group. Everyone silenced.

"Alright, alright. We will sleep here tonight. But, this place is not right. We will continue on in the morning. Fenn,

Lachlan, join me and Akemi. We will discuss procuring the Queen." Fenn unlinked his arm from Gwylfai quickly and followed the old mer to the back of the room. Lachlan, lingered for a moment longer and then reluctantly followed. He would much prefer entertaining the crowd than working on a plan with Earendil.

Soon, with nothing else to do, they hunkered down for the night. There were only a few hammocks available, and Gwylfai and Gwylin claimed them. Even though the room was bare, it was nice to be out of the open sea, where you always had to be on guard. Aerwyn slept wedged between Ula and Akemi, and she felt safe and happy. She drifted off quickly into a dreamless sleep. She must have been sleeping only a few hours when she was shaken awake by Lachlan. "Time to go" he mouthed. Aerwyn sat up, confused.

In the darkness, she saw Fenn holding a rope that was tied to a gagged and bound Queen of the Southerns. The little queen was wearing a gold plated and opal studded shark tooth necklace around her neck that glowed like an Eldoris.

Chapter 25: Beluga Blue

After a brief, silent search at the stables near the castle, they abandoned the idea of finding where the Southerners had whisked their arctic skates off too. Aerwyn felt a twang for the beast who had carried her so steadfastly from one end of the planet to the other. Hopefully he didn't become food. She shivered--he likely would.

They quietly swam away from the castle, taking care not to disturb the water too much. The Queen, who Aerwyn learned was named Muriel, put up quite the struggle for such a small mer, and it took Fenn, Lachlan, and Figgs to keep her moving. They hadn't been swimming for more than thirty minutes when Earendil halted them and ushered them to a bed of coral to wait while he left with Akemi.

Aerwyn looked at the bed--it showed the same signs of decay as the Lazarev castle. The spindles and spikes of the normally colorful coral were dull and stringy looking. There was a lukewarm feeling about the place--it did not have the vibrancy that a normal bed would have. Aerwyn didn't have much time to contemplate their surroundings further because Earendil and Akemi came back just a few minutes later. As they left the bed, Akemi explained to the group that they had awakened Tefnut, the mer who ran the ferry that traversed the West Wind Drift current. He would take them out of town.

Tefnut was the oldest mer she had ever seen. He was Pacificana originally, as he had gray hair that hinted of once being yellow, peach skin, and a blue tail. He looked incredibly excited, especially for being awoken in the middle of the night. He had already started preparing the ferry for the voyage when the group got there. The ferry looked like it had been awhile since it had been in regular use. According to Tefnut, who excitedly rambled on about the ferry's features as he prepared it to go, the ferry had actually been going on monthly voyages for years, even if there were no passengers to ride.

"Very excited we have some mers hopping aboard on this end! The other end, they like to use old Beluga Blue, but here, really don't get anybody. Come anyway though. Tradition and all that. But hop on board. We can get going soon. Very soon. I was prepping to start the trip back for the day after tomorrow anyway, so we are right on schedule. Yes, we will have to wait at the next port a bit because we will be early. But on schedule we are. Good thing you caught me! I really try to keep on the schedule."

The ferry was one of the most bizarre things that Aerwyn had ever seen. Upon close inspection, she could see that it was three blue whale skeletons stacked one on top of the other. The inside was encapsulated and kept from the rushing waters of the current by scavenged drift wood, which Aerwyn had never before seen, metal, and coral. There were six sails made of kelp sticking out 360 degrees around the frame, with the purpose of catching the current waters. A large paddle poked out of the back to steer the massive ferry. It was tethered to a large rock, and Tefnut was unwinding its tether at a sharp pace. As Aerwyn swam up to the entrance, a sheet of metal she had to slide to the side, she thought, here goes.

The first level, and whale skeleton, was the common room. There were plush anemone cushions surrounding short tables. The room well lit, with the glass orbs holding angler fish, lighting the room. There was a kitchen in the front that looked better stocked than the Southerns'. Once he loaded the supplies, Tefnut showed them to the rooms. The upper two floors had hallways that led to six rooms on each floor on the left side.

Aerwyn bunked with Ula, per usual. After she put her satchel on her hammock, she looked about the room. It was small but cozy. Her hammock hung above Ula's. Other than that, there was not much in the room except some worn but coral artwork and a closet with a few games and grooming items. She held the brush up to Ula and they both squealed with excitement. It had been days since they were able to take care of their matted hair and algae covered bodies.

Unsure of what Earendil wanted them to do, Aerwyn headed back to the main level. He was busy giving instructions to Tefnut. He nodded to her in his cold way, "We are about to be on the way Aerwyn. Settle into your room please." So, Aerwyn went back through the vertical hallway to the horizontal hallway that led to her room, passing Akemi, who was bunking with Muriel to keep guard. Akemi gave her a great big smile: "This is sweet!"

The next two weeks were some of the best of Aerwyn's life. There wasn't much to do on the ferry except eat, sleep, play games, and talk. Tefnut proved to be a fun and warm addition to the group, every one of which needed to take a break from the seriousness of their task. At this point they had been travelling for three months, and the strain of the travel, as well as the heaviness of the impending task, was wearing on everyone.

Muriel was soon revealed to be an easy captive. She was kept locked in her room, and the further they got from her home, the less worried they were about her taking off into the wilderness. Regardless, Aerwyn still dreaded when it was her turn to keep watch. Muriel was crotchety and bitter. She made many offensive anti-human comments, and no food or comfort was ever good enough for her. Her gold dust had worn off, so now she looked like she could be Puakai's grandmother.

The first port, the one that Tefnut had been so worried about missing, yielded no additional passengers, so the group was all alone during the first few days on the current. They even told Tefnut about the purpose of their journey--this was something Earendil had promised to reveal when bargaining for the last-minute ride. He was incredibly excited and supportive. As one of the last mers to travel from ocean to ocean, he knew that changes needed to be made.

On the second night, Tefnut regaled them with the history of the ferry. Years ago, there used to be ferries running on every current on the ocean, taking mers from ocean to ocean. As mers moved closer to the cities, after the Five had outlawed magic and interaction with humans, ferry travel slowed down. By the year 1950, it had stopped completely, except for Beluga Blue. And, as Tefnut pointed out, Beluga Blue only still ran because the passion of an old mer and not because it made any profit.

On the third night, they all drank too much dulse wine. Lachlan was the center of attention that night, regaling the mers with stories of Pacificana and his adventures there. Aerwyn noticed that he kept looking at Ula to see if she was listening, which amused her. He talked so loudly that there was no way that Ula could not be listening. He and Figgs had formed quite a friendship in the past few months, and their loving yet competitive way of comparing their two oceans caused laughs for the whole group. Gwylfai, Aerwyn observed, was seated once again next to Fenn. Her hair was perfectly smooth, waving around her shoulders like loose icicles. She had taken off her diamond necklace. Out of modesty? Thought Aerwyn. No, she probably thinks that Tefnut will steal it from her. Tefnut was not at all interested in Gwylfai though. He and Earendil could not stop talking to each other about the mission.

Aerwyn did notice that Gwylfai had managed to cover herself up where the necklace had been. She wore Gwylin's vest, made from silver strands and spotted with diamonds. Gwylin kept his white billowing shirt. Aerwyn knew how skinny he was under there--she had held him up as they escaped. She wondered if he had said something to Gwylfai about covering up. He was still pretty quiet, and he watched a lot more than the other mers. But Aerwyn thought he must have a lot to say. She looked forward to when he would say it.

Even Fenn seemed to relax. That third night, he kept asking Aerwyn questions about Atlantica and swimming competitively. Although interrupted several times by Gwylfai trying to turn the conversation to her, she was able to get in a rhythm talking with him that they had not been able to get too since the ball. It felt wonderful and right, like when her fins hit their stride during race. Fenn talked of Puakai, and how he hoped she could swim competitively one day. Aerwyn felt a pang of guilt, and once again wondered if she should tell him about the Vodianoi. I have time, she thought.

The fourth night, after just a cupful of the pleasant wine, she wandered up to the very top of the ferry. She found a hatch that slid to the side. There was a large lip made from driftwood that blocked the current from hitting her full in the face as she popped her head out. Her view forward was blocked by the wood, but she could see the vast expanse of the ocean plummeting behind the ferry at full speed. The fingers of the day's sun were receding into the ocean ceiling. She held herself up, easily resting her arms on the outside of the ferry. The view lifted her heart. After a few moments, she was joined by a red head, poking itself out next to her. Fenn had followed her up here. "May I join you?" He asked. "Sure." She replied.

The hatch hole was just big enough for them to rest side by side, but not big enough that their arms didn't touch. They watched the ocean roil by for over an hour, talking occasionally and enjoying the view. The places where his arms brushed hers tingled. Her one-hundred tiny braids, freshly done with the brush that she and Ula had found, flowed behind her as she breathed in the water through her gills. This was glorious. "You know, I miss Biscay a lot, but it is moments like this that make me think that I don't need it." She felt almost silly after saying it, especially to Fenn. Like she was a child, swept up in adventure, and not realizing the gravity of the task at hand.

"I know what you mean." Fenn replied, graciously giving her the benefit of the doubt. "It is a good look at what life could be like if we can save our homes and unite the five oceans again." He turned to her, causing her to instinctively rotate toward him. She felt a little embarrassed--once again, she felt like she wasn't savvy or serious enough. They were facing each other in the hatch, but a fin's length from each other. "You're… you're free Aerwyn. You're open. Open to so much. I wish I could be like that." He touched her arm purposefully then, running his hand down her purple skin. It took both forever and no moment at all for that hand to go from her shoulder all of the way to her fingertips. Then he dropped his hand and they looked at each other. She felt the push pull from him, and this time she could tell he felt it too. Their bodies moved ever so slowly, coming closely together. Then, a head popped out between them.

It was Akemi. "Hey mates, what's this? Wow. Check out that view!" and then it was three of them, looking out at the roiling ocean. But Aerwyn was smiling to herself and felt big inside.

Aerwyn had not yet told Ula about the ball. She worried that she had gained a poor reputation of not being serious enough and any discussion of push-pull feelings wouldn't help. Now she didn't want to tell Ula anything because wanted to savor the arm touch all on her own. She wanted to savor feeling understood and important by someone other than herself, and Coventina, of course, who was obliged to make her feel important.

The next morning, Fenn smiled almost eagerly at her when she sat down to eat breakfast. She smiled back and had to look away, because the smile would not break. It was like they had a secret between them now. A little arm touch of a secret. But the feeling didn't last long. Gwylfai plopped down next to Fenn, as she usually did, and Aerwyn's smile dropped.

"Oh goodness. This place is horrendous. I cannot wait until we are off of this forsaken whale carcass." She scooped up some fish jam and spread it on a coral cake. She took one bite and left the rest untouched. "I miss Arcticana so, Fenn." She said in her wispy voice, ignoring that anyone else was around. "You only saw a small part of the splendor of Arcticana. You would love it there. In the summer, we ride seals almost all of the way to the surface to find the freshest fish. And the sunlight there, in the summer, reaches to the sea floor all day and all night. It is like living in a crystal. We have so many diamonds. The whole city just sparkles all summer long." Fenn nodded along politely, just a tiny bit entranced by the white hair swirling around in front of him. She then rested her head on his shoulder as she babbled on about her ocean. To Aerwyn's surprise, he did not move. But Aerwyn did. She got up and left.

Chapter 26: On the Current

Aerwyn tried not to let Gwylfai ruin the time on the ferry, but her mind churned. I must have been confused about the ball. Why had I even thought there was something there? Just because I felt a push pull? Now I know he didn't feel that. He was just grateful that I saved his sister from the squid. It doesn't matter anyway... We are from separate oceans. Probably, I shouldn't want anything to happen--if I had any sense of self-preservation, I would have started with that thought.

Without Ula to talk to about this, she felt very alone. But, in an attempt to move on, she tried to shake off the whole thing. Instead of thinking about what the push-pull feeling meant, she threw herself into her friends. They had fun every day on the ferry telling stories, listening to Tefnut play his shells, lounging in the common area and making up games, and taking in the view at the hatch on top. It was a moment in time when there were no troubles, food was plenty and tasty, and learning about each other felt so good. Aerwyn forgot about the Vodianoi. She tried to forget about Fenn. Gwylfai's overt flirtations with him were not making that easy for her.

After a week on the current, they passed by a small settlement. To Aerwyn's surprise, it was, albeit sparsely, populated. Mers slid out from the doorways of their huts to wave at the passing Beluga Blue. The mers were from all over the oceans. Aerwyn even saw the white hair and silver body of an old Arcticanan tending his seaweed garden. Another few days went by and they passed another settlement. This time, when the ferry stopped, passengers got on. There was an old couple and a young mer man. The couple was originally Atlantican, and the younger mer was Pacificanan. He already knew Tefnut and was welcomed on warmly by the old ferryman.

One night, Aerwyn and Puakai were taking in the view of the sun's fingers receding out of the water out the top of the hatch, when Aerwyn felt the strong desire to tell Puakai about the Vodianoi.

"Puakai," said Aerwyn.

"Yeah?" the little princess replied.

"I need to tell you something about the uniting of the Eldoris."

"Yeah?" Puakai turned her attention to Aerwyn.

"The Vodianoi, he said that the uniting of the Eldoris might be dangerous."

Puakai shook her little blonde head in defiance, "Yeah, I know that."

"Well…" Aerwyn paused, unsure of how to proceed. "It might be more dangerous for you… because you are not fully formed yet."

"Oh." Puakai replied, working very hard to keep her face straight and the fear at bay. "Thanks for telling me that Aer."

The mers were silent for several moments before Aerwyn asked, "Do you have any questions? Do you want to talk about it?"

"Not really," said Puakai. "I've been kind of bracing myself… I'm not super surprised."

"Okay. Well I can talk about it whenever you want."

"Thanks Aer. Does Ula know?"

"Yeah she does."

"Good," said Puakai. "Aer?"

"Yeah?"

"Don't tell my brother okay? Wait for me to? I'm worried he will freak out."

"Okay, Puakai."

Suddenly, they found themselves engulfed by orange. It was everywhere, and momentarily stopped Aerwyn's breath. But as soon as it happened, it was gone. Hands pulled them down. It was Tefnut, the stranger, and Fenn. "I was looking everywhere for you Puakai!" Snapped Fenn.

"It's okay, okay," counseled Tefnut, as he patted Puakai on the head. "You see young merman, she is fine." He turned to Aerwyn. "That's a phytoplankton bloom. Saw it coming a few minutes ago. Those blooms, they come on fast. Had to close up some of our windows. It will clog your gills all up real fast. Has killed some mers before." Aerwyn nodded. "But," he lifted something Aerwyn had not seen him holding, a large bowl-shaped glass, "Put this on your head and you can take in the view for a few moments at least."

Aerwyn looked at Fenn and Puakai. "No, thank you Tefnut, my sister and I are good." Puakai looked disappointed, but didn't put up an argument. She understood that she shouldn't be taking any risks. Aerwyn on the other hand was curious and excited to get back out there.

"Sure!" She said with enthusiasm. Tefnut showed her how to put the bowl on, and she, Tefnut, and the stranger took turns popping their heads out of the hatch to take in the glowing orange mist floating all around them.

That night, all of the passengers, even Queen Muriel, crammed in the common room, and Tefnut played his clam shells for them. The old couple started dancing right away, and Aerwyn watched them twirl around in the water, with a foggy haze around her from the wine and food. After the first song ended, the stranger, who Aerwyn had spent the day with in the orange mist, asked her to dance. Why not, she thought. Soon most of the mers were twirling around to the music, dancing with each other. Fenn did not dance, and sulked in the corner. Aerwyn was happy to see him shake his head when Gwylfai came up to him. She sat down next to him instead, which did not make Aerwyn happy. Eventually Puakai grabbed her older brother by the hand and dragged him onto the dance floor. Aerwyn couldn't help but laugh watching Fenn spin Puakai around with a smile growing on his face. Puakai, without fail, seemed to melt away his standoffish exterior to reveal a warm, kind mer underneath. Aerwyn wondered why he was so guarded, but was beginning to understand that it came from his desire to protect his sister.

The new passengers refrained from asking the group any questions, which was a relief, and they were respected as fellow wanderers. Aerwyn felt like she could live life this way, perhaps, if she ever stopped missing Coventina so much. After his dance with her, the lone stranger kept trying to get Akemi to dance with him. He's swimming up the wrong reef there, thought Aerwyn, remembering Akemi flirting with the snow-haired merwoman in Is.

Soon, Tefnut played a classic Pacificanan song and Aerwyn leaned on Ula's shoulder as they watched the Pacificanas, even Earendil, put their arms around each other, swaying back and forth, and listened to them sing the song of their people.

Oh ours is the largest of the seas

Pacificana is home to me

Swirling green waters and storms a plenty

Swimming our ocean is a risk times twenty

We've fought Poseidon's enemies

And brought to our Queen many glories

Oh Pacificana

Home to me

Fenn flopped down next to Aerwyn grinning. "Aw, the good old Pacificana!" Together they rested and watched the rest of the dancers. As the night became late, the fog in Aerwyn's brain grew thicker, and she slowly nodded off to sleep.

She didn't know how long she had been sleeping with her head on Fenn's shoulder, but, as she looked down, she saw Puakai resting her head on his lap. The music was still going, but only the old couple were still dancing, and they were dancing very slowly. Aerwyn felt a thrill at touching Fenn. He hadn't shrugged her off or anything when her head fell there. In fact, he was sitting so still as if not to disturb her. Maybe he was asleep, she thought. She turned her head and peeked up at him. Nope. His dark eyes caught her looking at him, and the skin around them crinkled in a slight smile. Aerwyn turned her head back and caught someone else's eye, Gwylfai's, staring at her with disdain. When Aerwyn smiled at her, she tossed her head and looked away. Aerwyn only felt a little bad about smiling.

Fenn carried Puakai up to bed. Aerwyn followed them up, since her room was right next door. She felt a pang in her heart watching Fenn's strong arms hold his sister so gently. All of a sudden, she had a resolution. I have to tell him about what Callan said. I don't care what I promised Earendil or Puakai. He has to know. She swam the hallway a few times as she waited for Fenn to come out. She waited until Fenn closed Puakai's door and was floating in front of her in the narrow hallway before she spoke.

"Fenn," she almost whispered. The push-pull was strong now, and they both seemed to float toward each other. Fenn didn't reply. He reached out his hand and touched her hip slightly with his hand. He leaned his head toward hers, their eyes never breaking, slowly… there was a crash in the hall near the stairwell. Figgs and Folander were rolling in the water laughing. They roughhoused their way past Aerwyn and Fenn, completely unaware that they had ruined what Aerwyn thought was going to be a moment. She laughed nervously. So did Fenn. She waited a second to see if he was going to proceed with the moment, and he didn't do anything. So she spoke. "Um, Fenn, I have to tell you something."

"Yes?" he asked, his grin slightly mischievous. His dark eyes held hers and she wanted to be close to him again. He appeared to not know what he wanted to do, and just floated there, so she marched on.

"Fenn, I have to tell you about what happened with the Vodianoi." His grin dropped.

"Earendil told me that Callan gave him directions to the spot to unite the Five." He responded quickly and almost defensively.

"He did do that, but… he also told us something else. Something that I promised not to tell.

"What? What is it Aerwyn?"

"He told us about how unsafe the uniting could be… that there is some risk."

"Yeah, I know that." He whispered back briskly.

"I don't know if you know all of it… the risk isn't equal to all of the mers performing the spell. Mers who are not fully developed yet, the young ones, are at the greatest risk. Puakai, she is so little... she... she could die." Aerwyn whispered.

Fenn was silent for a moment. He ran his hand through his magnum colored hair. "Why didn't you tell me this sooner Aerwyn? Back when we were at the bottom of the Pacific, close to my home?" Then his voice raised above a whisper, "Wait, were you ever going to tell me?!"

"I told Puakai." Aerwyn responded.

"You told Puakai?"

"Yes, it... it is up to her after all."

"You told an eight-year-old mer that she is most likely going to have to die to save the ocean, and you put that on her?" Fenn, swam away for a second, and then swam back. "What in the hydra were you thinking?!"

"I... I just thought she deserved to know."

"What about me? I'm responsible for her Aerwyn! I am the one who needs to keep her safe."

"Yes, but it is her life... she gets to make that choice." Aerwyn, tilted her head up a little, sticking to her guns.

"She is eight!"

"She is, but she is smart and strong. Talk to her about it and counsel her... but you have to respect her choice." Aerwyn replied. She put her hand on Fenn's arm, and he shrugged it off.

"Where do you get off keeping this information from me? It is so easy for you to swim here, having nothing at stake, and try to comfort me that my sister has the choice to die. Why didn't you tell Earendil no? Or make him tell me? I thought you were my friend!" Fenn whisper yelled, pulling at his hair.

Aerwyn felt anger at that. It was fair for Fenn to be mad at the situation, but to imply that she did not say anything until now because she was afraid of Earendil was another. Especially since she had been thinking about the right thing to do for weeks and striving to do it. "Do not, Fenn, for one moment, confuse my kindness for telling you now as any sort of weakness. And, do not confuse my compassion for attempting to be there for you as a lack of standing up to others. I thought this through. I wanted to do the right thing. For everyone."

Fenn looked at her with a weird look on his face, and then, much to Aerwyn's surprise, he pulled her close to him with one hand on her waist and kissed her, deeply and strongly. Aerwyn sunk into the push-pull for just a moment, feeling his body close to hers, his muscles tight. Then, a voice popped into her head. It was Coventina. "Always ask for what you want, and say what you don't want." Years of going with the flow because she was too polite to say anything just landed on her shoulders all at once. How dare he kiss her after being so rude and questioning her motives? This was not how she wanted this to go, no matter how strong his mouth felt on hers.

She put her hand on Fenn's chest and pushed him back. He stared at her with dark eyes. "Fenn," she said quietly and quickly, "I don't want this." He said nothing and immediately turned and swam away. "Fenn!" She whisper-called after him, trying to keep her voice low. But he didn't turn around. As she hovered in the hallway outside Puakai's door, she whispered to herself "I meant, I don't want this like this… like this."

Chapter 27: A Missing Eldoris

Aerwyn woke up the next morning feeling exhausted from tossing and turning the night before. She didn't want to tell Ula about what had happened. Somehow, even though she was proud that she had said what she wanted, she thought Ula would laugh at her for how it all went down. Aerwyn tried to laugh at it, but her heart hurt at the thought of it. After the fact, she was really very shocked that Fenn had kissed her. Beyond that one night at the ball, in the several months they had spent together at this point, she hadn't received a lot of clues about his feelings. I know that he caught me looking at him a fair amount... but had he been looking at me as well? It was probably all ruined now. She thought. But, I will try to talk to him. It is nothing that a little explanation can't fix. She wished she had some means to speak with Coventina. If only she could see her now, defining how she wanted her personal interactions to go! Her grandmer would be so proud.

It proved to be very difficult for Aerwyn to give Fenn that little explanation. He was nowhere to be found at breakfast, and he spent most of the day in his room. The following day was not fruitful either. He appeared to be avoiding her--not looking at her during meals and turning around and leaving if he came upon her. On the third day after the incident, Aerwyn thought enough is enough, and she approached Fenn, who was sitting with Lachlan and Figgs.

"Fenn, um, do you mind talking with me for a sec." Lachlan and Figgs gave Fenn a funny look, and Figgs, to Aerwyn's embarrassment, said "oooooooh."

"I can't right now," replied Fenn tartly. To which Lachlan gave him an exasperated look and elbowed him in the ribs. Fenn stubbornly remained seated.

"Okay, well, anyway…" said Aerwyn. And, seeing no other option, "I'm sorry about the other day. What I said wasn't the whole thing." She paused, and he appeared more interested in his shrimp than her, "The whole thing is… well… It's just not that easy…" When Fenn still didn't look up, she gave Lachlan a tiny smile, which he returned. "Okay, well never mind then." She said, gathering her pride, "it doesn't really matter," and she swam off. She heard Figgs saying "come-on mer, don't just leave her hanging. That one is a good one." To which she thought she heard Fenn say sheepishly, "I know."

The next day, the ferry passed through a hot spot, and the temperature of the entire vessel changed so much that the mers could actually feel the warmth. This was the signal for the final stop for regular passengers. There were quite a few passengers at this point. As soon as they cleared the hot spot, Tefnut unloaded everyone off of Beluga Blue. Earendil had arranged to pay Tefnut extra to take them privately up the West Australia current, which would be another four days ride, and drop them right at the seat of the Indian Ocean. The mers, although originally grateful for the rest, were getting restless to make it to their next destination.

Aerwyn took the opportunity to leave the ferry and stretch her fins. She and Ula swam through a seaweed patch, letting the smooth grasses run over their bodies.

"It is so good to stretch my tail!" exclaimed Ula, swimming in a somersault. "I feel like it has been ages."

"I know," replied Aerwyn. "It will be good to get to the Indian Ocean… I'm growing weary of travelling in such close proximity to everyone."

"Oh really?" said Ula, arching an eyebrow. "Everyone… or just Gwylfai?"

Aerwyn turned her head sharply to look at her friend. Perhaps Ula was picking up on more than she realized. "I don't know what you mean." She responded, still not ready to talk about what happened on the ferry. The mers made their way to the edge of the seaweed patch.

"I don't know," said Ula, pushing the grass aside, "It's just that she seems to be all over Fenn, and I thought…"

"Ugh. Fenn. He is so haughty and severe. They deserve each other," called Aerwyn loudly, as if to convince herself of it. With that exclamation, she emerged from the seaweed patch. There, alone and treading water, was Fenn. "Oh," she said.

"Never mind then," he said as he turned and swam quickly away.

Ula peered out of the grass, next to Aerwyn. "Do you think he heard me?" Aerwyn asked.

"I don't see how he couldn't," Ula responded quietly, looking at her friend with a concerned look on her face.

"I'm fine Ula," Aerwyn responded, "let's get back to the ferry."

The two mers rejoined their group, and made their way back onto Beluga Blue for the final leg of the journey. They all settled into the common room, thankful that there were no more outsiders to hide their purpose from. Just as Tefnut was rotating the sails and the ferry was about to take-off on the turn up the West Australia Current, Ula swam furiously into the common room. "Earendil! I cannot find my crown… someone has stolen it!" She exclaimed, breathing heavily through her gills. "And they left this note in its place." She proceeded to read the note to the group, which had gathered around her.

"Dear **PRINCESS**, I know who you are. Good luck uniting the Eldoris without yours. Keep the humans out. Sincerely, A Concerned Mer."

Everyone looked aghast. Some more than others. Aerwyn and Ula were upset for the loss of Ula's valuable possession, but they didn't have the same gravity of emotion that the unknowing others did. Earendil uttered a long "no," along with some other garbled words, and sunk to the ground with his head in his hands. "We are ruined!" He exclaimed. "Without the Eldoris, we have nothing!" Fenn, on the other-hand, had that same look of relief mixed with guilt that he had when they had come upon the deserted Lazarev.

Akemi, Lachlan, Figgs, and Folander immediately started strategizing about how to find whoever took the Eldoris, "but there were twenty passengers!" Ula and Aerwyn exchanged a look, and Aerwyn nodded and tried to convey with her eyes, "I think we have to."

"It's okay everyone" said Ula, "everyone!" but no one was listening to her in the chaos of trying to solve their problem. "EVERYONE" she yelled, and all heads turned toward her. "It was my crown that was stolen, not the Eldoris."

"But I thought that the crown was the Eldoris… that is what Queen Ulayn told me" Earendil said, hope and confusion dancing together on his face.

"Yes" replied Ula, looking at Aerwyn, "But actually that wasn't true." Everyone looked confused, and maybe even a bit betrayed. "Aerwyn has the Eldoris… it is her coral necklace… the one she dropped in the jellyfish swarm." Everyone looked at Aerwyn in silence. Aerwyn was eternally grateful for Ula mentioning that it was the one she risked everyone's lives to go back for. She smiled awkwardly and held up her necklace in such a way that, when she thought about it later, she was embarrassed.

"Ahhhh" said Figgs, breaking the silence, "I thought you were being a little silly to be going back for a necklace! Makes sense now though…"

"What a relief!" Said Earendil, gathering himself up to a floating position again. He continued sharply "If anyone else has anything to say about a decoy Eldoris, we need to know now. We should have no secrets in this group if we are to succeed." Aerwyn looked again at Ula, this time rolling her eyes, as they both knew Earendil was keeping the secret of the Vodianoi from the royalty in the group.

"No decoys here" purred Gwylfai, speaking for the first time.

"Same here" answered Muriel, "you ruffians made sure of that."

During the whole commotion, Fenn was just looking at Aerwyn, with his mouth slightly open. It almost made Aerwyn laugh. Well, at least that issue was cleared up. She wasn't a total useless idiot, and her queen had trusted her enough to carry the Eldoris. Now they all knew that.

"How did anyone even know that there was Eldoris on this ferry anyway?" Asked Lachlan, interrupting the collective relief.

Earendil immediately snapped, "That is what I want to know! Did anyone talk about what we are doing?" He demanded. Everyone shook their heads, murmuring of course nots and nos.

Tefnut coughed nervously. "I told the Pacificanan that you were on a quest." All heads turned to him. "He must have guessed… I thought I could trust him. I'm so sorry everyone. I put all of your efforts in jeopardy!" The old mer started to cry. "What can I do to make it up to you? Oh dear, I never in a million years thought he could guess."

Earendil sighed and put his hand heavily on Tefnut's shoulder. "Old friend, we should never have included you in this mess." Then, turning to the others, he continued, "the damage is done. We must thank Poseidon that these Atlantican merwomen deceived us all. In the end, it was a wise safeguard. He must have taken Ula's crown because it is… was… the most valuable item on this whole ship. I wonder who else's belongings he rifled through?"

"I did notice him lurking near Muriel's room a few times when I was guarding it," interjected Akemi. "I thought he was trying to flirt with me again… I bet he thought she would be an easy target, not wanting to be here… and having few belongings so that it would be easy to pick out the Eldoris."

"He also was lingering near my room," Gwylin said quietly. This was the first time he had spoken to the whole group. "I thought he was looking for my sister, which is not uncommon," he smiled apologetically.

"We need to start keeping a watch out the hatch, in case he is serious about not wanting us to succeed and has decided to follow us. Tefnut, no more passengers." Earendil ordered. Tefnut nodded somberly.

After that, the trip on the West Australia current went quickly. With the ferry to themselves, the mers worked on their plan for the final stage of the quest. First to the Indian Ocean seat, Cocos, and then onto the site to unite the Eldoris, the Great Barrier Reef.

Soon, they were docked at the outskirts of Cocos and saying goodbye to Tefnut. With minnows in their stomachs, they slung their now thin satchels over their backs and headed toward the city.

Chapter 28: The Coral Ocean

It was immediately apparent to Aerwyn that magic was still alive in Cocos. The waters were warm, and the corals were the brightest that Aerwyn had ever seen. They were everywhere, on every surface of every rock and sand mound. The mers that Aerwyn saw were also the most colorful she had ever seen. Their bodies and fins were patterned in bright colors, and their hair was a shade of their bodies. Unlike the other tribes, these mers didn't all look similar. The only feature that bound them together was that they all were patterned. Among these patterned mers, Aerwyn saw the gold skin of Southern defectors, a few Pacificanans, Atlanticans, and even two Arcticanans. There were several mermagicians milling around as well. Earendil swam next to Aerwyn as they entered the city, and he explained that the mermagicians of the Indian Ocean were not regulated like in the other oceans. Here, they could use their powers for more than just healing, as long as they used their powers for good. So many mermagicians immigrated to Cocos.

The mers were greeted warmly by the Indiansi, who waved and smiled but were otherwise unfazed by the travelers. No wonder mers from around the world settled in and outside of Cocos, it was a welcoming mecca for all types of mers. Small, bright homes carved into the coral, with stained glass windows and rows of beads floating down across the doorways speckled the path into the city center. It was a stark contrast to the Southern Ocean's sandy ruins and the Atlantic Ocean's bleak caves. Aerwyn felt her spirits rise by just being around the bright cheeriness of the community. It looked as if these mers hadn't faced hard times. If they did, they ignored them and strove onward with cheeriness.

The palace rose out of the city center like a mother gathering her merchildren toward her. It was low lying compared to the other palaces Aerwyn had seen, as it was a hollowed out coral reef on the sea floor. Aerwyn could tell it was the palace because of the colorful seaweed decorating every pointy surface, like flags. The long seaweed pieces reached far away from the palace, floating gently in the current. It gave the effect of a very large crab, swaying in the water. The party was greeted at the door by two mers with the black and white swirling stripes of the lion fish on their tails and torsos.

Ula and Aerwyn stayed tight by each other's sides. Since the theft, Aerwyn felt a duty to be more vigilant regarding her best friend's safety, and Ula was on edge since that invasion of her privacy. Their alertness did not stop them from opening their mouths in awe upon entering the palace. Every surface on the inside was a vibrant color. There were red corals, pink sea anemones, yellow coral statues, barnacles painted in a rainbow of colors, blue tubes with luminescent algae radiating light, and beads strung everywhere. It was color, vibrancy, and energy. It was chaotic. Aerwyn had a passing feeling of discomfort with the chaos, but quickly adjusted. She was in love. She looked at the faces of the mers around her. Gwylfai looked disdainful. Of course, thought Aerwyn, this is too much for her plain, luxury aesthetic. Muriel looked grouchy and envious. Aerwyn's fellow Atlanticans looked awestruck. She snuck a peek at Fenn. Once again, his face was unreadable. Puakai, at his side, had her hands clasped with pleasure.

They passed through the reef with ease and were led to the great hall, where the Indiansi queen was waiting for them. She was sitting on a throne of a thousand different colors--corals, meticulously grown into the throne shape, weaving in and out amongst themselves. The queen was about Ulayn's age. A chubby mer, apparently her husband, sat next to her. To Aerwyn's surprise, their thrones were placed at equal height. He gave the group a large smile when they entered. Their bodies were magnificently colored. The queen had the blue and orange pattern of a mandarin fish, and her husband had the large white and orange stripes of a clown fish. Each was wearing a crown of a simple strand of pearls, and each had simple pearl earrings in each ear. Aerwyn made a mental note of this tastefulness and thought Gwylfai should as well. Who needs ornamentation when your body alone is so flashy.

The queen greeted the mers, spreading her arms wide. "Welcome my friends from across the oceans. You have made it to Cocos, the seat of the Indian Ocean, acceptor of all and home of the outcasts. I am Queen Darya, and this is my other half," she smiled lovingly at the chubby mer at her side, "Dathan. If you will please make an appointment with our staff," she pointed to a zebra striped mer, "they will inform you of the plots in Coco that are available for your settlement. We will help you as much as we can." She then turned to her husband and resumed her conversation with him.

Earendil coughed politely. "Your majesty, we aren't here to settle" he started. The queen looked back, quizzically. Looking at the mers more closely this time.

"Go on" she replied, interested.

"We are here as a contingent of mers from all the oceans" Earendil continued. Aerwyn thought she heard a quiet "herrumph" come from Queen Muriel. "We are on a quest to unite the Eldoris using the power of the royal female line. We seek to break the barrier between land and sea. We are going to expose ourselves to the humans and make them see what they are doing to our oceans."

"That's the quickest I have heard that," Ula whispered to Aerwyn, who grinned back in return.

It was soon apparent why Earendil was so short winded with his plea. Dathan shot upright, and Darya grasped the arms of her throne. "Finally!" Dathan said quietly and hoarsely. The Indiansi had been waiting for this day.

Darya made a few quick orders "Guards, attendants, all out while we dispose of this nonsense. Ferdirad, you stay." Aerwyn's heart fell, watching the attendants scatter. When everyone was out besides Darya, Dathan, and the bedraggled group, Aerwyn's confusion was lifted as the queen spoke openly.

"We have been waiting for this for so long! Each year we have sent out a messenger to each of the seas asking for cooperation in contacting the humans. Each year, we get answers back that dishearten us. We have a mermagician researcher here, Ferdirad, who has been trying to figure out the way to break that barrier without all of the Eldoris…" With that, Ferdirad nodded solemnly to the group in a way that indicated he had not had any luck. "But, what you are saying is that you have brought the Eldoris here?! And the royal lines? I see Pacificanan, Atlantican, Arcticanan, and even a lone Southern. Are we your last stop?"

"Yes," replied Earendil. His voice was suddenly tired and full of emotion. Aerwyn had not really thought about this being Earendil's life's work before. No wonder he could be a bit intense.

Queen Darya rose up next to her husband as he spoke. "We have much support here in Cocos for breaking the barrier. Our ocean has been warming for much time now. We farm as much as we can, but food is becoming scarcer. We have been recording our crop output for over 100 years... these last ten years have yielded a disastrously low crop that we just can't sustain on. The reefs that make our homes are fading in color and dying. There is garbage everywhere here. There is a floating garbage patch that blocks out all light. We never know when it will hit. We are without light for days at a time. Yes yes yes we will help you unite the Eldoris" he spoke passionately, and put his arm around his queen.

"We do not have any children, yet" continued the queen, placing her hand on her belly. Aerwyn hadn't noticed the bump until then--Darya was pregnant. "But, I will do it." Aerwyn looked at Earendil. Was he going to mention the risk to this woman? Would he risk the life of her unborn child? He said nothing and nodded.

"We can be ready to go tomorrow" Dathan said, his arm still around his wife. "We will gather just a small group. I don't want to draw notice. Although many in our ocean would support breaking the barrier, those who don't support it feel very strongly. I wouldn't want to put any of us at risk."

With that, Dathan swam back to the queen's throne and broke off a small piece of coral from one of the decorative spikes. He held it up for the group to see--it was a pure white iridescent carving of a sea horse. It gleamed with magic like the rest of the Eldoris. "We are going to need this!" he exclaimed.

Chapter 29: To the Reef

To Aerwyn's disappointment, their stay in Cocos was short. They had a quiet dinner with Ferdirad while Queen Darya and Dathan organized their preparations. The food in Cocos was very spicy and flavorful, and Aerwyn could not help but take three helpings. When she reached over for her third helping of curried caviar, she evoked the first smile from Fenn that she had seen in a long time. She took it as a peace offering and smiled back, scooping the spicy delicacy onto her plate. She would have loved to explore the city, roam the trails through the coral, and eat more of the delicious food, but they had to be off the very next day. Earendil was very uneasy after the theft of Ula's crown and wanted to get going at once.

Aerwyn had a restless sleep in her colorful room in the castle. Her hammock was hung between two tall spikes of coral, and the coral was interwoven so much here that she doubted there were actual walls to her room, just closely grown corals of every type and color Aerwyn had ever heard of. The room was lit by a human chandelier, floating down from the ceiling. The room also had a table and two chairs, retrieved from a shipwreck. Aerwyn really liked how the Indiansi incorporated their neighbors from the land. Not ignoring them but using the great things that they made. She was once again sharing a room with Ula, who seemed just as restless as her.

After what seemed like hours of not being able to fall asleep, Aerwyn drifted into an uneasy slumber, only to be awoken way too soon, feeling groggy and poorly rested. It was Akemi, poking her head in the door. "Mermaids," she whispered excitedly, "It's time." Ula and Aerwyn sleepily stuffed their meager belongings that had made it this far into their satchels. They had re-braided each other's hair last night. As Aerwyn looked into the human mirror, eyeing her three long braids and shabby vest, she got the first good look at herself since the ball. She had grown very muscular, and her face had sharpened the way it does when you are constantly stressed. She felt fierce, and she liked it. She looked at Ula, who was wearing her one braid wrapped around her head several times. Ula also looked more muscular. But Aerwyn also noticed that she did not look as confident as before. She had a haggard, hanging back look. Aerwyn swam up to her and put her arms around her.

To Aerwyn's surprise, Ula cried. For several minutes, she quietly wept on Aerwyn's shoulder while she stroked her back. When her friend finally stopped crying, she didn't move from

Aerwyn's arms. "Aerwyn," she sniffed, "I don't want to die." Aerwyn pushed her out at arms-length.

"You're not going to die Ula. The Vodianoi's warning was for the weaker mers… for the old and young and sickly. You are strong. You're going to be able to do this." Aerwyn told her friend, believing her words. "Plus, you've got me, and I'm not going to let anything happen to you. I'm clearly the best person to have on your side on this vacation." She nudged her friend to laugh at her reference to the first night of the quest. But Ula was serious when she responded, "No, you wouldn't. You're the best Aerwyn." Aerwyn felt warm inside.

No wonder I feel tired, it is not even dawn yet, Aerwyn thought as they waited outside the castle side door. Everyone was there, yawning. But beneath the tiredness there was a jittery apprehension. It was if their bodies sensed the closeness of the task that had not long before seemed so distant. Several Indiansi combers joined them, leading behind them what appeared a human canoe led by a long log of driftwood. As she hopped in with her satchel, she saw on further inspection that it was a long hollowed out piece of coral with a curved current guard on the front. The mers sat three by three in the canoe, which was being led, to Aerwyn's shock, by a giant moray eel, and not driftwood. She eyed the eel's sharp teeth warily. One of the Indiansi must have sensed her apprehension. "They're tame." She said. "They have been raised from birth by us."

The eels were fast, and the canoes made great time through the water. No one said much as the early morning rays grew in the water, signifying the start of day. It was a straight shot through the Timor Sea to the Great Barrier Reef. Ferdirad had informed them that it would take just three days, and that they weren't going to stop. Folander sat to the left of Ula, and Lachlan sat to her right. It seemed very important now that nothing happen to her. Akemi and Fenn flanked Puakai, Gwylin and Figgs, much to his pleasure, flanked Gwylfai in the canoe right behind them, and Aerwyn and Earendil sat on either side of Muriel. The tiny queen was no longer tied up as she had quit struggling days ago. Aerwyn wondered at the ethics of making a mer go through this when she didn't volunteer, but it appeared like Muriel had resigned herself to her fate. There were only a few Indiansi joining the mers. Dathan was there next to his wife, and a guard sat on the other side. There was Ferdirad, the mer who told her about the eels, and then just one other merman, who looked very fierce. Aerwyn sat right behind Akemi, but the now friends didn't talk. No one talked really that first day. Nor the second. Nor the third. The minnows in Aerwyn's stomach were becoming uncomfortably large.

By the morning of the third day, Aerwyn's body was exhausted from sitting in the canoe. Her eyes were exhausted from looking at the scenery passing with such speed that they couldn't catch hold of anything. Her mind was exhausted from trying not to think about what was going to happen to Ula. What she wouldn't give to be out there flipping around and stretching her fins. By noon, she was sure she was just going to scream out and demand that they stop. She was sure others must be feeling the same way. Finally, when she was sure she couldn't take it anymore, and the scream was coming at any time, they stopped.

As the mers untangled themselves from their unnatural seated positions and slowly started going about the process of setting up camp, Ferdirad led Earendil through a grassy wall, and they were lost from sight. Dathan explained to the group that the site to unite the Eldoris was right behind the grass wall, and they were going to camp here to have the royals rest up in order to unite the Eldoris at first light tomorrow. Aerwyn felt both curious and anxious about what was behind that wall. Ula nervously hung by Aerwyn as she set up camp.

As they set up camp, it became evident that mers had been here before. Old hammocks were strong from coral, and generations old dishes were scattered about. When Aerwyn had strung her hammock, she was able to take a moment to look around. The reef was astounding. Even though she would not have thought it possible, it was more colorful than Cocos. There were stacks of corals of every color of the rainbow surrounding the alcove in which they had chosen to make camp. Fish were plenty here as well, and their colorful bodies flitted around the towers of coral, paying their guests no mind.

Ula nervously wandered about all afternoon. Finally, right before dinner, she sat next to Aerwyn. "Distract me Aer. Anything. Please."

Aerwyn looked sympathetically at her friend. "Okay Ula. Well… I can tell you something embarrassing. Will that help distract?"

"Literally anything," responded Ula desperately.

So Aerwyn told her friend about her feelings for Fenn. How she had been mistaken about him. How loving he was to Puakai, and how torn he was about his mother. She told Ula how he noticed the good parts of Aerwyn that no one had noticed before. She also told Ula about the kiss, how she rebuffed him, and how afterwards she thought maybe he thought Gwylfai would be an easier mermaid to pursue.

"Oh Aerwyn!" Ula responded, when she was done with her story. "I wish you had told me this sooner!"

"I know… it just didn't seem right to make a big deal out of it… considering…" Aerwyn waved her hand at the group gathered and helping themselves to dinner.

"But Aer. I heard Fenn on the ferry. I heard he and Gwylfai in the hatch… they didn't know I was there." Ula rushed. "He rejected her Aer."

"Oh… but that doesn't mean anything" said Aerwyn, but the hope in her voice made her feel transparent.

"He said he had feelings for someone else. Gwylfai told him that she had heard about the kiss, and that it sounds like that wasn't going to work out. Fenn said he didn't care… he said he was wrong to kiss her in that moment… and that it was his fault. That he had blamed her for something that wasn't her fault… That was you Aer! He was talking about you."

Aerwyn was silent, the hope that had filled her moments before burst through her body as it became happiness.

"It all makes sense now…" continued Ula, "I would have told you instantly if I had known. I mean… I thought you might but…" But Aerwyn wasn't listening. It had all just been a misunderstanding, she thought. And then he heard me say those terrible things in the seaweed patch… of course he wouldn't want to say anything after that. Her mind whirled. She needed to see him. To talk to him about it. As Ula continued on, oblivious that Aerwyn had stopped paying attention, Aerwyn's eyes searched for Fenn. They found him seated next to Puakai, helping her cut-up her dinner. He handed her a small piece of fish and then tenderly placed his hand on the back of her head.

"You've got to tell him Aer," Ula's voice brought her back to the conversation. "He should know how you feel."

Aerwyn looked at the brother and sister, making the most of the last hours of the day. Maybe their last day. "No, Ula. Not now." Ula looked where Aerwyn was looking. "We have to focus on the Eldoris. This can wait." And even though it truly felt like she couldn't wait another moment to hold Fenn and tell him how she felt, she knew she had to.

Chapter 30: Uninvited Guests

As they ate a hearty and flavorful meal packed by the Indiansi, Earendil and Ferdirad went over the plan for the next day. All would rise right before sunrise and the ceremony would begin once the first sun ray filtered into the water. This was important, Earendil explained, because the sun's transcendence past the barrier weakened it just briefly, or so Callan had said. Earendil also explained that the reason they had to do it here was that this was where the most humans dove under the ocean's surface, vacationing and researching wildlife, constantly crossing the barrier, and weakening it just a little. The non-royalty would be placed in strategic locations surrounding the ceremony, keeping guard.

While the mers processed this, they tried to keep conversation light. Lachlan kept pointing out to Ula all of the various kinds of fish that were not native to Atlantica, that she had never seen before. She gratefully engrossed herself. Fenn was somberly sulking, while Akemi and Puakai played a game of urchin spikes. Gwylin and Gwylfai were leaning on each other, watching the fish swim by and talking about home. Aerwyn felt bad for Muriel, all alone, so she tried to ask her some questions about Lazarev. She was given such cold responses that she eventually gave up her attempt to be friendly.

Soon it was dark, and time for bed. Going to bed before the day to unite the Eldoris was unsettling. It felt like the night before Poseidon's Feast, except the anticipation of joy was replaced with anticipation of the unknown. Aerwyn's stomach felt weird and, despite being exhausted from the canoe ride, she had a very difficult time falling asleep.

Aerwyn did not know she had fallen asleep until she was awakened by someone putting a hand gently over her mouth. She could tell by the green blur in front of her that it was either Figgs or Folander. He held a finger up to his lips to signify that she should be quiet. Aerwyn's eyes quickly adjusted to the dark of the water, and she saw the other mers poised in various states of awakeness. No one was moving. Lachlan, who had been on watch, was breathing heavily, and bubbles were jetting from his gills. Aerwyn could tell that he was whispering to Earendil, because his mouth was moving, but she could not hear anything at all. Earendil beckoned Akemi to him, said something, and then flicked his hand for her to spread the word. She went to Fenn first, whose face went aghast and he slowly moved his hand toward the spear that was resting in his hammock. When she made it to Aerwyn and Figgs, they had

265

already gotten the gist--there were mers out there. Aerwyn was shocked when she heard Akemi whisper in her ear "It's Pacificanans."

Aerwyn rooted around for her spear clumsily. She grabbed a hold of it and sucked in her breath. Were they going to have to fight? This she was certainly not going to be good at. Before Aerwyn could even fully process what was going on, Earendil was whispering orders. "Akemi, Lachlan, you stay behind with the royalty. Guard them with your lives. Everyone else, come with me." Aerwyn nervously held her spear, bouncing it in her hand, and looked around. Ula and Darya were armed, the other three royal merwomen were not. Puakai had a quivering lip but was holding her head up bravely. Aerwyn nodded to Ula and took off with the rest of the mers in a silent swarm, not allowing herself to think about it.

They passed through the outcrop of coral that protected the alcove and nearly bumped into a mass of blue tailed mers. There was no hiding themselves now, as they were face to face with the Pacificanans. When Aerwyn stopped short with the others, Fenn was by her side. "Mom." he whispered. Aerwyn turned her eyes in the direction that Fenn's stricken face was pointing. There, guarded by several heavily armed mers, was a long, statuesque mer with short flame orange hair sticking out from beneath a crown of starfish. "Mom!" He exclaimed, loudly this time. Queen Puk Puk turned her face toward her son, but her eyes remained blank. There was no indication in her expression that she knew who Fenn was.

A mermagician emerged from behind her. "Earendil. Traitor of the Great Ocean, so we meet again. I was so hoping that it wouldn't come to this," he said in a silky voice. Earendil said nothing. "You met my associate," he continued, indicating a mer next to him. It was the stranger from the ferry. "Thanks to Kai here, we were able to make the short trek across the South Pacific just in time. We lost your tracks after Arcticana, but our talented network of combers did not let us down." Earendil didn't say anything and looked stone-faced at the mermagician. The mermagician continued. Aerwyn tried to take in what he was saying, but she was also trying to count how many Pacificanans there were. She counted 22, but started over to make sure. They had just nine in the fight with the royalty left behind and two mers guarding them.

She snapped back to the conversation when she heard Earendil say: "By no means are we going to tell you where the princess is. And, by no means are we going to hand her over to you. Her decision is final." Aerwyn looked to Queen Puk Puk to see if she had any response to the mention of her daughter.

There was nothing but an empty stare. She heard a quiet, guttural sound come from Fenn. She reached out and grabbed his hand. He squeezed it tight.

"Then we have no option but to regain our princess by force and halt this preposterous and dangerous task." The mermagician waved his hand, beckoning the troops behind him to swim up. "You're a crazy old mer Earendil, and your discontent with our Great Ocean will be the death of you." He raised his staff. "Mers," he said in his silky monotone, "kill them all and bring the princess to me."

Chaos erupted. The Pacificanans hurled themselves at the tiny group, and the tiny group hurled themselves back. Figgs whooped out a battle call as he joined the fray, and Folander laughed wildly. They were made for this moment. Their spears moved wildly in the water; their tails hitting the second blow.

Soon, Aerwyn found herself in hand-to-hand combat with a Pacificanan almost twice her size. She had a brief out of body moment where she thought of her shark defense training at the Academy and how poorly suited she was for this type of spear fighting. She was quick though and able to stab him in the fin and flit off to a mer more her size. She tried not to think about the repercussions of the stab. Stabbing and flicking and swimming, she moved around the mob, just trying to stay afloat. The swarm of mers was soon emitting swirls of blue blood like a spinning whirlpool. Aerwyn saw one of the Indiansi fall to the sea floor, Dathan rushing to his side.

As she battled she saw Folander take a spear to the arm. It was quickly becoming evident that they were outnumbered and, no matter how skilled, were in a losing battle. Aerwyn chanced a glance upward. Queen Puk Puk hovered above it all with a blank stare on her face. Fenn was fighting his way through her guards, trying to make his way to her. One of the guards drew a long human sword from behind his back. It looked like the kind Aerwyn had read about in her human novels. It glimmered in the water, as the guard swung it around his head.

"Fenn! Watch out!" she yelled, pointing up at the sword. Fenn had just enough time to duck. Next, he adeptly flicked his tail, knocking the sword out of the guard's hands and sending it hurtling through the water.

"Cheater!" He yelled, as he punched the guard in the face.

Earendil fought his way to Aerwyn's side. "Aerwyn," he rasped, out of breath, "We have got to do it now." He stabbed a Pacificanan in the gut. "Herrrumph" he groaned as he pulled the spear out. "Come with me! Now!" Aerwyn frantically disengaged herself from the mer she was fighting. "Ferdirad, hold them off as long as you can!" Earendil shouted across the fray. Ferdirad gave a whoop in response and started stabbing with reinvigorated energy.

Aerwyn followed Earendil back through the coral outcropping. They were greeted by a fierce Lachlan and Akemi, whose faces softened upon seeing them. They hardened up again quickly when Earendil shouted "Now! We do it now! Lachlan and Akemi, join the others--hold them off at all costs!" Lachlan and Akemi left to join the fray without hesitation. The merwomen waiting gathered themselves up quickly and followed Earendil through the grass wall. Aerwyn took a deep breath and took up the rear.

Chapter 31: Change

The grass wall was thick, and it took several long moments to break through to the other side. It was immediately apparent to Aerwyn that they were in a spot where magic could happen. There, in a pure white sand clearing amongst the coral reef was a circle of five corals. The corals were thin, almost too spindly to be standing upright on their own, and about 10 tails tall. There was a blue opaque coral, a silver glittering one, a green iridescent one, a gold one, and one with a swirling pattern of many colors. Aerwyn had never seen corals like this before. It clicked in Aerwyn's brain--each coral represented an ocean.

But she didn't have time to take any of it in. Earendil was pointing the royalty to their places. All looked nervous, but had brave faces on. Gwylfai's face was serene and composed as ever. Puakai held Ula's hand between their two corals, and both were grimacing. Even Muriel swam up to her gold coral with some determination. It could have been that Earendil had threatened to kill her if she didn't participate. Aerwyn didn't know. She chose to believe that Muriel wanted to do the right thing.

Darya put a hand to her pregnant belly and spoke, "Merwomen--we have taken upon us a momentous task to try to make our world better. Bear-up and find strength these next few moments, for you will need it." And with that, Aerwyn could actually see each merwoman turn inward and, a moment later, turn outward with more determination.

"We must do it now!" Shouted Earendil. "Everyone, grab hands in the circle while I recite the incantation." He pulled a small stone tablet covered in runes from his satchel. "We should be able to break the barrier with this combined power. We don't have time to wait for daybreak." The mers in the circle grabbed each other's hands.

"No!" Fenn shouted. Aerwyn turned, he must have followed them in here. He burst into the clearing. "Puakai, you don't have to do this!" And, before anyone could stop him, he swam swiftly into the circle. He grasped Puakai's shoulders. "Puakai! Mom is here. She is different. She's not mom. You can't go too. I can't lose you too Puakai!" He sobbed.

Puakai put her hands on either side of her brother's face, "you won't lose me, brother. I am strong, and I have my friends to help me through this" she said, motioning to Ula and Gwylfai on either side of her. "But you have to let me do this. Now go. Listen to your queen." Fenn let go of Puakai, grief-stricken. Earendil grabbed him and dragged him out of the circle.

"Grab your Eldoris!" Earendil continued, keeping an eye on Fenn to make sure he wasn't going to swim into the circle again, unmoved by his pain. Aerwyn ripped the iridescent coral from her necklace and handed to Ula.

They all had their Eldoris in hand--the coral, the starfish, the chambered nautilus, the gilded shark tooth, and the sea horse. One by one the merwomen readjusted their grasps on each other's hands, now holding the Eldoris between them. They lifted their clasped hands to the sky. "NOW!" Shouted Earendil, and he began loudly chanting in a language that Aerwyn had never heard before.

Aerwyn and Fenn swam around outside of the circle, completely helpless and unable to assist their fellow mers. After a few seconds of Earendil's chant, the Eldoris started to emit little rays of light. Aerwyn's eyes widened as she watched. The lights from each Eldoris seemed to be reach for each other. Bit by bit each strand of light lengthened. Soon, the lights were meeting at the middle of the ring. They twisted with each other to create one bright strand.

"Keep going!" Shouted Earendil. Ula's face was screwed up with the effort of holding the energy of the Eldoris steady. The other mermaids had similar looks on their faces. Puakai started to tremble under the effort.

The twisted light grew and grew, away from the mers and towards the surface of the sea. Then, it stopped growing, and remained twisting, just several tails away from the surface. Aerwyn looked at Earendil. He was still chanting, but a panicked look had come across his previously calm features. She looked back at the mermaids. She saw why Earendil was concerned. Puakai was shaking with the effort. She had fallen onto her fins and was struggling to hold the Eldoris up. Her arms kept dropping. Gwylfai and Ula were the only reason why her arms were still raised. Fenn was right behind her, watching helplessly and calling her name. Puakai's skin started turning white. Aerwyn looked up. The barrier wasn't weak enough for them to break it. Where was the sunrise!?

All of a sudden Aerwyn felt very far away. She thought she heard Fenn telling Earendil that the spell wasn't working and Earendil responding that they must keep going, but their voices didn't seem real. The whole world dropped away from her, besides the colors of the Eldoris. Then there were images flashing in the water in front of her. There was a human baby swimming in the water with little legs and a mat of black hair. There were the smiling faces of humans looking down at her. There was a ship, sinking to the sea floor. The humans were drowning. There was a young mermagician woman holding the baby with the black hair. It was Coventina. Now the baby had a little purple tail. The images came on so fast, that Aerwyn didn't know she had slid to the sea floor in her shock.

Aerwyn came-to with Fenn by her side looking at her worriedly. The fog of her vision melted away, and she looked back at the circle. Now Ula was also white and on her fins in the circle. She shook her head to rid herself of the fog. She heard Figgs' voice. "Earendil, we can't hold them much longer!" Now Earendil was by her side, pushing Fenn away.

"Aerwyn," Earendil said with an eerie calmness. "Aerwyn. It is time to tell you… You're…"

Aerwyn interrupted him--the vision had made so many things very clear to her. Her different looks, Marna's warning, why Ulayn wanted her to go on this trip. "I'm a Changed." She stated.

Earendil nodded and bent down on his tail, speaking to her kindly "This is it Aerwyn. We can't seem to get through without the weakening of daybreak. We are almost there, but I'm afraid much more will kill all of our merwomen. I think you can get through, being a changed. But… I don't know if you can survive it. I don't know if you can get back. I'm sorry I don't have those answers for you."

Aerwyn looked at her friend and the other brave mermaids struggling nearby. She looked at the beauty of the reef, of her home, the ocean. She thought of Coventina. "What must I do Earendil?"

"Follow the Eldoris."

Aerwyn swam to the outskirts of the circle. She looked at Ula and gave her smile of love. To Aerwyn's horror, Ula was past the point of recognizing Aerwyn. She then looked around the circle for Fenn. After he had left her side he had swam back to Puakai. His hands were tearing out his hair.

As she swam into the center of the circle, she thought she heard him call her name and yell "no," but she was too focused on her task to tell for sure. She looked at him, and his eyes were deep. She felt the push-pull of him asking her to stay back. That look felt like it lasted her whole lifetime and permeated every cell in her body. She wished he knew how she felt about him, but the time for that was over.

She broke her eyes away from him, and then she swam resolutely into the light of the Eldoris. And then up.

Aerwyn's head broke through the barrier and into the air of the humans. She gasped for breath and kicked her legs to stay afloat as the waves crashed around her.

Made in the USA
Monee, IL
12 June 2023